T0156836

CIRCUMSTANTIALITY

mariam anwari

iUniverse, Inc.
New York   Bloomington

Circumstantiality

iUniverse books may be ordered through booksellers or by contacting:

iUniverse
1663 Liberty Drive
Bloomington, IN 47403
www.iuniverse.com
1-800-Authors (1-800-288-4677)

Because of the dynamic nature of the Internet, any Web addresses or
links contained in this book may have changed since publication and
may no longer be valid. The views expressed in this work are solely
those of the author and do not necessarily reflect the views of the
publisher, and the publisher hereby disclaims any responsibility for
them.

ISBN: 978-1-4502-4581-4 (sc)
ISBN: 978-1-4502-4582-1 (ebook)

Library of Congress Control Number: 2010915433

Printed in the United States of America

iUniverse rev. date: 10/08/2010

cir·cum·stan·ti·al·i·ty
3. A pattern of speech that seems to wander because of excessive detail but eventually reaches its goal idea.

(The author credits Merriam-Webster's Medical Dictionary with the above definition of "circumstantiality." *Merriam-Webster's Medical Dictionary.* Merriam-Webster, Inc.)

Dedicated to my mother, Gul Anwari. Without her love and support this work would cease to exist. Thank you, Mom. Thank you for being my everything.

Chapter 1
Brian

Sometimes people still ask what it was like to be his roommate.

Still.

After all this time. It's been many years and for some reason no one seems to want to forget what happened to Charles, except his family of course. And me. I guess that's the world though. Everybody loves a good tragedy. Watching the high and mighty take their falls. For some reason, people love that.

Sometimes if I'm drifting off long enough, I can hear him laughing.

Still laughing at me.

*   *   *

I was eighteen years old when I got accepted into Princeton, the university where I would meet Charles as my roommate. I still remember the walk down the hallway into our dorm room, the first time Charles and I would meet. It was my first year at the University and I was going to be the roommate of the

1

son of one of the wealthiest men in our country. My family lived on Stratton Street. Charles' family lived on Glen Falls Drive. If one were to compare our respective neighborhoods to a Monopoly board, I would be stuck somewhere on Baltic Avenue, Charles undoubtedly perched on Park Place. If you wanted to look at it that way...

Stratton Street was considered to be pretty much in the slums of our town. Ancient buildings rundown apartment complexes and homeless people loitering around decaying corner shops. Nothing truly horrible, and nothing very notable either. Unless someone were to find the occasional drunk vagrant shouting in the streets about how he shouldn't have trusted his whorebag of a wife Millie with his money in the dead of the night notable. The Mayor used to gently refer to the neighborhood as *Old town,* adorning our festering side of the tracks with a nickname of charm...charm and authenticity. It might have comforted some of the residents into believing that their homes and schools and jobs were located in the heart of town, the only true-blue remainder of our city, untouched by technology and newfangled architecture, but I wasn't one of them. The only authentic thing in our neighborhood were the damned storefronts, fading, eroded, having been the exact same for the last forty or fifty something years. I didn't think Charles Gardensen and all his grandness would even know that Stratton Street existed. He ended up surprising me on that one. It was the first of many surprises in our friendship, anyhow.

I spent my youth growing up with just enough, never more. My mother didn't need to lecture me any; I knew what happened to people who spent their lives screwing around. They lived all around us. I saw it every day in the eyes of the listless cashiers, the sluggish stockers at the department stores, the gum-chewing sales associates at the Salvation Army. Eyes glued to the clock. Eyes filled with apathy, regret. Eyes drifting far over me, over the scanning of an old sweater with a slight hole in the sleeve, over me counting the exact change in my hands, far over me, somewhere I can't see. People whose qualifications didn't stretch over a napkin. I was well aware.

My mother's routine chidings throughout my adolescence were more than mere words; they were the people I saw every day. She raised me single-handedly. My father disappeared before I was even born, which was too much of a cliché in our situation to even allow us to pity ourselves appropriately. If she missed him, I never knew; she acted like he never existed. The two of us formed an invisible wall to the world around us, shutting out the painted-up girls with short skirts, the needles on the floor, the people sleeping in doorsteps. Even at a young age, watching a neighbor once dig through a trash can to fish out a battered pair of shoes, try them on, and then walk away in them, I knew. I had to do something. I had to get out of... this. Perhaps at a very young age, I knew this right away.

And so I played smart. Studied my ass off. Year after year of pencils, books, tables, charts, index cards, and the occasional Playboy magazine stuck in between the folds of a thick textbook. Area. Integral. Derivative. Thesis. Onomatopoeia. Hemingway. Darwin. Newton. Habeas Corpus. Jefferson. Franklin. Brahms. Daguerreotype. Rule of Thirds. I knew those -I knew them all. I knew the only way out of this apartment, this neighborhood, and the inevitable shitty customer service job at minimum wage would be based on one thing and one thing only: my education.

I had no other connections whatsoever.

My mother knew this earlier than I did, and I think that's why even at a very young age she thrust me so strongly into my education. When other six year olds where watching *The Power Rangers* and playing Cops N' Robbers, I was given a battered packet of Flash Card Math and a 250 piece jigsaw puzzle. When you only got one card to play, you play that card. You play it damn well.

I ended up as the Salutatorian when I graduated High School. Got accepted into every university I applied to, full scholarships all around. My mother was so proud. Looking back, I wish I had given myself more credit. I brushed away the compliments, handshakes, and honors- in my mind I wasn't even close yet. I was only interested in the next step, growing up, getting the fancy degree, walking out the door and making a success out of myself. Looking back now I wish I had relished my youth a bit more. Spent more time being a kid. Consequently, I never truly had any friends growing up. Many nights were spent indoors, alone, with a library book tucked under my arm. Other nights I'd spend hours battling the antennas of our ratty television, trying to get a few clear stations. Sometimes I just lay in bed, imagining I was hanging out with the popular kids from school doing...whatever they did for fun. Like I said I didn't really have friends, ergo I didn't really have any girlfriends. Imagination was required in that area as well.

My mother noticed my loneliness some nights, and when the air must have been particularly potent with it, she would knock on my door and offer me five dollars from her faded little clasp purse. "Brian, I passed by a few shops on Main Street and they're having some great sales on books and other knickknacks like that. Maybe you can meet some friends down there?" I would smile, and sometimes I went. Sometimes I didn't. The older I became, the less I minded. I suppose even at a young age, I understood the weight of my choices, and the sacrifices that followed them. With each passing year, each delighted teacher, each flawless report card, each promise of being able to polish a future to my liking...well, it was going to be worth it. Right? It was going to save us.

I'll never forget the day the letters from colleges arrived. One after the other, congratulating me, accepting me. Congratulations... I read that word for what it really meant. *Congratulations: This is your ticket out.* A feeling I'd never forget. It was going to be the first time in my life that I truly had choices. Not just the dry noodles, a dime a package. Not being given the hand-me-downs. Not the same pair of shoes for three years now. Not having to deal with assholes in junior high and the even bigger ones in high school laughing at me, because of my clothes and shoes were either two sizes too big, two sizes too small, or simply falling apart. There would be no more of that, not for much longer. Holding the letters in my hand, reading that one word over and over again, the satisfaction was immeasurable.

I paced around the living room for hours, waiting for my mother to come home. When she finally turned her key in the lock that night, already muttering about how tired her feet were after a double shift at the beauty salon, I merely smiled. And waited. Waited for her to turn and ask me if I've checked the mail yet, because my college replies should be in the mailbox any day now, and if I could please throw a package of noodles on the stove because she was starving. Simply smiled and waited, until her eyes fell on the coffee table where I had spread all the letters over. She dropped her bags and ran over.

And screamed. Over and over. I swept them all up and began reading the acceptances out loud, one by one, tossing them over my shoulder as I went onto the next one. Her screams grew louder as the colleges became more prominent.

I laughed. "Mom, mom, calm down," I remembered saying, trying to hug her. I knew her excitement would exceed my own. She wriggled around as I tried to hold her still.

"Which one, Brian!? Which one?! Which one are you going to?!"

I sat her down and held her hands. Told her I had thought long and hard about it and decided I was going to Princeton. It was only one state away. I didn't want to be too far from her, in case she needed me. I didn't like thinking about her being all by herself while I was gone. Besides being one of the top ten universities in the country, Princeton had also recently added a graduate degree for neuroscience, something I was embarrassed to admit I had been fascinated with since ninth grade.

"Princeton!" She cried, tears of happiness shimmering in her eyes.

Later in the privacy of my room that night, when I was absolutely sure that she had fallen asleep, I cried too.

Just the month before I was scheduled to move into my dorm, I read in the local newspaper that Astin Gardensen's son, Charles, would also be attending Princeton in the fall.

The Gardensen family was considered the pillars of our society, semi-celebrities, if you would. Astin Gardensen made his fortune importing and exporting product overseas, an extremely seasoned businessman who had settled in New York. Astin was in the papers time from time. Mostly after completing some highly lucrative business deal or other. Sometimes they ran features on him, articles recognizing him and his family for donating hefty sums of money to charities, fundraisers, libraries, shelters, and certain universities. Since his donations were never less than in the multi-thousand dollar range, those in power of our town garnered quite an amount of respect for Astin Gardensen. Other than his financial wizardry, all else we really knew about Astin Gardensen was that he was married with two children, his firstborn son Elijah, and another boy, two years younger, my future roommate, Charles.

The only time Astin was ever in the papers non-related to finances, it was to report the tragedy of his eldest son's death. The news managed to travel across the country; Elijah Gardensen was found dead in their home at eighteen years old. Something about an accident at their home or other, at the time I couldn't remember the details so well. The community held a memorial for him, lasting for three whole days. After his memorial, Astin disappeared altogether from the business world. A few papers tracked his whereabouts in Europe, in South America, and after a few years he finally returned to America. Astin eventually resumed his successful enterprise, reentering the business world, continuing to make successful deals and donate munificent sums of money, (mostly directed at organizations for children at that point) while his wife Adele and Charles quietly went along. Or so the story went.

Not only three weeks before I was scheduled to move in, I learned that Charles Gardensen would be residing on campus as well. And only a week after that, I learned that I was going to be his roommate. Me. The son of the most influential, powerful, well-regarded and wealthiest man in town, someone I strived to be like, his son would be my roommate. When I read his name next to mine on the residency papers I had to pick up, I thought it was a joke. An error. My roommate?

Charles Gardensen? The Charles Gardensen? The millionaire? Why would Charles Gardensen choose to live in a Princeton dorm instead of some... private suite? Or his own apartment? House? Condo? It was a surprise not only to me, but to everyone who came to learn of the news as well.

When I remember all of this, I sit back and wonder what our lives would have been like, which directions they would have turned had we never met at all. Most of all, I wonder what Charles would have done that night all those years ago, had I not been there.

CHAPTER 2

Charles

Somewhere, in my mind...way in the back, behind all the screaming, shouting, breaking glass, endless games, toys, money, girls, meaningless one night stands, whispered words behind my back, solitude, emptiness, fights, cars, presents, outbursts – me just, absolutely fucking losing it- behind the uncertainty of... myself, I try to believe... I'm innocent. I'm innocent. I wasn't always like this. I was pure once. Just like you. I was pure.

*   *   *

To be perfectly honest, college wasn't originally in the cards for me.

I know what you're thinking, life deals you a hand, and you play it. Or some shit about lemons, and making juice, I don't know. What you don't know is that if *I* don't like the cards, all I do is get another deck. And let life deal me another hand. And another, and another. Until I'm ready to play.

It's not a luxury most people in this world have, I know

that much. I was born into the wealth. The wealth so many envy, the wealth so many struggle for, the wealth which people do unspeakable things for. Things that can never be taken back. Yes, I'm well aware. I know I have enough money to never have to work a day in my life. Enough to never have to go to school. Enough money to stay inside and dream all day. And what does a multi-millionaire's child dream of? I don't know. Perhaps, finding meaning in a world that seems to have none.

At first we loved it – me and Li. My older brother Elijah. Our lives seemed perfect. We were constantly occupied, bought out with the latest toys, fashions, movies, electronics. We were constantly passed from one set of hands to another, playing under the supervision of a different pair of eyes each hour, it seemed like. Bought out and therefore we were too busy to detect the silence between our parents. The silence, the beautiful distractions they fed us, my father always away on some business trip. We didn't notice it so much in the beginning. We weren't looking for it.

What I did notice however, even early on, was the way Astin would say goodbye to us before he'd leave for work, or one of his seemingly endless business trips. It was always the same, Elijah and I would run to the door, seeing him off. And Astin would always turn around, signal for the driver to wait, and then take Elijah in his arms, smile at him, kiss him, mess with his hair. And when it was my turn, he would give me a short smile, pat my head, and walk out the door. It was only when I was older; I noticed the difference between the smiles he flashed at Elijah, and the ones he forced for me.

Elijah was the family favorite. The Son who could "Do no wrong!" He was just the fucking chip off Astin's block.

God, how much they loved Elijah, my parents. It was quite sickening, actually. By the time I came around, three years later, he had already found everything he wanted in a son in Li. I was nothing special. And knowing that at a young age, maybe that's what did it. Took away my innocence. Maybe that's what made me the way I was.

I've always found human nature funny. For instance, ever notice how much you want something when you know you can't have it? That one never gets old. It was ridiculous how much I wanted Astin's approval, his admiration, his love, his...anything. When I saw Astin look at Elijah, love literally emanated from his eyes. Whenever he happened to look at me, which was truly seldom, really, I saw...nothing. Cloudiness. Those gray eyes would glance at me, and he would smile, but they'd be far away. Not with me.

And so when I figured out was nothing special to him, I acted accordingly. And eventually, I went from being nothing special to being a pain in his royal ass. I got too old for toys, eventually. Unlike Elijah, I didn't make the standard transgression into a blossoming adolescent ready to take over the family business. No. In fact, the last thing I wanted to do was grow up and be Astin, married to my business and living in and out of suites from country to country. I started sneaking out. If I didn't have access to all the money I wanted, I would've stolen from Astin, just to spite him, but it was never a problem. I started smoking. Cigarettes first, then marijuana. But I ended up hating it, feeling all slow and sleepy. That's not my thing. I was much too restless to sit around with all my thoughts, all the thoughts smoking weed brought me. So I stopped smoking it, but never kicked cigarettes. I Invited anybody and everybody over to the mansion when he wasn't there. Wrecked my room. Charged thousands of dollars of useless, forgettable merchandise, clothing, toys, trinkets, to his accounts. Stole expensive alcohol and cigars from him, usually imported from other countries. Drinking was different. I liked feeling loose, liked the carelessness it gave me, the ability to forget Astin and his approval. The ability to forget Elijah's death, the past, myself and smile at everything. I got wasted and didn't care. Bought insanely extravagant presents for girls whose last names I didn't bother to get. Disappeared from home for days at a time, until he would finally give up and call me and demand me to come home. And you know what the fucked up thing is? I don't know which was better. Being nothing to him, or something…something that constantly bothered him. The proverbial thorn in his side…just something he didn't want.

I try to tell myself, it wasn't my fault. When I fucked up things, I was just trying to get him to love me.

Elijah understood. He would come home, find me trashed, sometimes messing around with some girl, would find the plethora of jewelry and shopping bags tucked under her coat, and grit his teeth. I knew it drove him crazy, but he always managed to keep it inside. He'd then escort the random girl out and come back drag me into my room. He'd talk to me. Ask me why I wasn't in school. Ask me if this is what I intended to do with the blessings I've been born with. Ask me why I didn't try to have any real friends. He would stay with me until I either fell asleep or started vomiting. He never got mad. He understood. Somewhere in his heart, he knew it too. He knew Astin loved him much more. He didn't understand why, but he knew.

Elijah's handsome square jawed face was framed in almost

every hallway of the mansion. Until the accident. She couldn't handle looking at them after that. She made me take them all down.

And how scary it was, seeing his face, over and over, as I pulled down each picture. Staring at me. Finally understanding why.

*   *   *

I never had any real friends growing up, the obvious reason being the wealth. Sure, I had friends. People I went out with, paying for the entire bill at the restaurant, and buying all of our tickets at the amusement park, and there were people who came over to use my latest video game console, or watch movies on my flat screen. I always had people around me. I guess you could say I had a hard time trusting them. I still have a hard time trusting people. I think it scares me. The fact that you can never really know somebody, you know? Never.

Doctor Langley was the one who recommended college. *Doctor* Langley. My mother likes to call him that, instead of what he really is which is someone who slept through years of psychology schooling and makes three hundred dollars an hour to ask me how I feel about everything under the goddamn sky and pretend to care about it. Told my mother and Astin that being around large groups of people my age, people with goals, trying to establish their lives and identities would be healthy for me. A few years dedicated to activity and studies, recreation would be a good step for me. Perhaps I would discover a hidden talent or knack for a subject. Find myself some hobbies. He even thought the separation of me from my family would make us realize how much we love each other. I laughed. I told him my mother was so doped these days up I was surprised she could still recognize who I am He told them he hoped I could do it there, make a strong, emotional, mental, connection with somebody. Make some friends. See, that was my problem.

"You don't seem to have any friends, Charles."

They hoped I'd make a friend. Someone to "Be there for me!" Join the Chess club, even. Debate. Be passionate about something. Date a girl steadily. Or at least for two weeks.

"Sure I do, Doc."

Of course I needed to be somewhat close to home, for security purposes, and the Doctor thought that me knowing that my home wasn't so far away would be comforting, (despite the fact that I told him the further I was away from my parents, the better) and so they had me apply to Princeton.

"Charles, a man's biggest influence is not his mother, father, sister, or brother. His biggest influences are his friends."

Well, apply isn't really the right word. It's more like, Astin made a few phone call to his good friend, the president of the school, and had someone do a bunch of paperwork, and bada-bing, I was enrolled for the fall semester.

"Doc, Astin is one of the richest men in the country. He and my mother hate each other. They don't know what to do with me. My brother is dead. I caught the last twenty people I tried to make friends with stealing from me on a regular basis. I think I'm pretty fucking "friend" repellent. Going to college is supposed to fix that? Acting like 'one of the regular' kids? Maybe I'll get to play beer pong and go to a football game? And then everything will be fine?"

My mother cried when I left. What her tears were made of, I don't know. Guilt. Sorrow. Regret. I wish I knew. She couldn't tell me even if she tried. Oh, my mother. My mother my mother my mother…

"You keep saying how important Elijah is to you. Wouldn't you think he wanted this for you? To at least try?"

My mother is a very beautiful woman. Even now, even angry at her, I can say this about her. And her beauty is not one of years of plastic surgery and tweaked out lips and ridiculously augmented breasts and annual face-lifts or anything ghastly like that. No. Her beauty is incredibly soft, incredibly vivid. She's very delicate, with a long slender neck. Her eyes are very big and very brown. Very deep. They are, perhaps, her best feature. Her mouth is small, her lips plump. She always looks like she's going to say something, but then thinks better of it and keeps her lips shut. Her skin is very pale, and is the softest touch I can remember from my childhood. And no, she isn't 25 while Astin is 63 or anything like that. They actually, believe it or not, married for love. She was with him before business made his millions.

And Astin, good old Astin Gardensen. When it was his turn to say goodbye, he stood at the door to see me off. I remember standing there, waiting for something. Waiting for a reaction. I was too tall for him to simply pat on the head now. I wasn't a child blinded by toys anymore. I was a grown man, awaiting goodbye from the man I called father. I was an adult, and I could see insincerity when it hit me. I stood there, I stood there. It felt like forever, but I stood there, feeling nothing. Feeling like crying. Wishing the bastard would hug me.

Instead, he drew a key from his pocket and placed it into my hands. I looked up.

"A college present." He said simply.

I stared outside, through the window. It was raining. Parked near the fountain was an electric blue Porsche coupe.

"I know blue is your favorite color. " He added, after a minute, hands in his pocket again.

I felt a cold smile stretch over my face. "Blue was my favorite color fifteen years ago. Just for the record, it's now green. Maybe if we had more than 2 conversations a year, you would know that. But that's okay, there's always the next car, right?"

He pressed his lips together forming a tight line on his face and put a hand on my shoulder. "I really hope this time in school goes well for. I want you to know that your mother and I will provide you with anything you need to do well there. Go to class. Learn something. You might be surprised."

I stared at the key in my hand and felt nothing, saw his hand on my shoulder and felt nothing, felt absolutely nothing fill me up, expand me, felt nothing rush through me. All I could feel was the cold metal of the key in the palm of my hand. The key in my hand. All I could feel.

The cold metal was the only thing I felt the entire two hour drive there.

CHAPTER 3

Brian

I remember moving into Princeton like yesterday. The campus was beautiful; up until that point in my life it was the most impressive place I had ever been. I had only seen pictures of it in the brochures sent to our old apartment when I had first applied. While the pictures were obviously made to be very appealing, the real thing was so much more powerful.

I walked through the vast campus, taking in the dark gothic buildings covered in ivy, enchanted by the air of regality emanating from them. I looked down at my rooming papers, trying to remember where I was scheduled to live. *Hamilton Hall.* I was scheduled to move into room 357. After a myriad of wrong turns down the elegant, long, and seemingly identical hallways of the building, I found it at one of the last doors on the third floor. My hands hurt from carrying luggage through to compressed hallways, filled with wandering students, the walls echoing with their excited jabber. I was relieved to finally set everything down. I fished the room key I had been given out of the good pocket of my jeans (the one without the resewn bottom) and suddenly froze before the door, wondering if Charles Gardensen had arrived yet. Was he inside? I felt a tinge of nervousness pass over me just as a rushing student bumped past me, successfully knocking her suitcase into my knee. *Ow.* I bent down to rub the inevitable bruise, suddenly feeling very tired and just wanting to sit down. I stared at the heavy wooden door, the gold stenciled numbers, *357,* my future on the other side of them.

Here we go.

Turning the key in the lock, I kept my eyes on the floor. I decided to stamp my shoes clean before walking inside, a pathetic attempt to alert anybody inside the room that I was about to enter it.

No response.

I cleared my throat.

Nothing.

I looked up.

No one around. But he had been there all right. My pupils must have dilated an inch; the front room we were supposed to be sharing was immaculately dressed, equipped with far more furnishings than I knew the school would ever supply. I mean, really, he went *all* out.

Large paintings in expensive looking frames hung off of every few feet of the walls. He enjoyed eclectic artwork, paintings done in all crazy shapes and colors, things of that sort. It wasn't as fancy as I would've guessed for the likes of a Gardensen, but as I would later come to find out all Charles really shared in common with his wealthy family was a last name.

An incredibly beautiful, dark, gothic-looking bookcase stood in the corner of the room, leather-bound books lining its sleek shelves, little porcelain and crystal ornaments stacked neatly alongside. I spotted a fountain-ink dipped pen, and its inkwell, initialed, *C.G*, on the center shelf. *Well, well, well, initialed fountain-ink pens*, I mused to myself. *Classy fellow.*

A desk, made of the same dark upscale wood as the bookcase, decorated the far right corner of the room, sunlight spilling over its sleek surface. That's one thing I remember truly loving about Princeton, how no matter what time of the year it was, when you walked through the campus, sunlight flowed abundantly through all the windows and tree branches down onto wherever you happened to be standing. Even in the dead of winter (my least favorite season), the mornings were so beautiful and bright.

A lone crinkly piece of paper laid upturned on the desk, as if someone had carelessly deposited it there. I walked over towards it, glancing over my shoulder to make sure no one was around, and turned the paper over.

It was a class schedule. *Psychology 101, Introduction to Philosophy, Introduction to Theatre,* and *Sociology.* And then there it was...I was still surprised every time I read it. His name. *Gardensen, Charles L. Freshman. Fall Semester Class Schedule.* I shook my head in wonder, placing the paper back as I had found it.

Walking through our housing unit, I felt like *Aladdin* in *The Cave of Treasures*, wanting to see and explore everything, scared to touch anything. He certainly had a lot of little knickknacks and ornaments. Untamed exotic looking plants in crystal black vases were perched on the windowsills. Well, exotic enough to someone whose garden is surmised of dead grass, anyway. I peered closer at them, recognizing the plants as Pothos plants.

"Devil's Ivy." I affirmed, out loud, to an invisible audience.

I turned to my left and let out a thick exhale. Along with his knickknacks, Charles Gardensen had brought many other splendid commodities. I stood there gaping, facing an entertainment center. Television, DVD player, stereo system, the shelves packed with CD's and DVD's. All complete with black leather couching. *Here are the first perks of rooming with the rich,* I thought to myself. *What nice shit!* My mother and I never had leather couches, and certainly not an entertainment center. We didn't even own a DVD player. I couldn't wait to tell her. Come to think of it, that moment could have very well been a snapshot in a *"What doesn't belong here?"* puzzle, with me as the obvious ragged fallacy.

I flopped onto the couch, sinking into its delicious softness. The soreness in my back seemed to dissolve and the rich smell of real leather filled my nostrils. *So this is what it's like,* I thought, submersing myself in its exquisiteness. I spotted the remote atop a classy looking dark wooden coffee table, and clicked the TV on. A menu guide for what seemed like a thousand channels popped up. I had only heard about this kind of stuff in commercials. Was this for real? I stared at the remote, trying to figure out how to work it. After messing with a few buttons, I managed to start flipping through the channels. Cooking. Women's Entertainment. Animal Planet. Travel. Music. Fitness. American Classics. Opera. Action movies. Romance. Horror. History. Cable on Demand. Spanish TV. It was endless.

"Jesus, how many channels are on this thing?" I asked myself in surprise.

"About 200 on that particular setup, I'm afraid." A voice said from behind me.

Shit!

I stood up quickly and flicked the TV off. *Damn it, damn it, damn it. Here I am sitting on his couch, flipping through channels on his huge television like I've known him for years.*

"Sorry about that, I didn't mean to ah, touch your things." I quickly dropped the remote onto the couch. "No one was in here when I came in, and uh, they're very nice. It's a very nice, ah, setup you have, here..." This was it. Our first meeting. I lifted my eyes off the floor and used the opportunity to look him over. Here was Charles Gardensen.

I don't know what I expected, but he seemed annoyingly spot-on as to what every wealthy, successful man's son should look like. Charles was tall and built slim. He had that thick, fine dark hair, healthy looking as hell, probably from…organic everything. The kind of hair my mother always wanted me to have, instead of my wavy mess of locks.

He also had that flawless, unblemished skin, obviously having skipped out on all the "Acne Years," which so few guys our age managed to escape. Piercing blue eyes. A dramatic mouth, full lips. Defined jawbone. He was a good-looking guy, if I had to admit it. Very healthy looking. He wore a dark brown leather jacket over a simple dark navy dress shirt, and black dress pants. Very simple in design, very high in quality, as was most of his wardrobe. He offered a slim hand, a hand that probably had never suffered a blister in the entirety of his life.

"I'm sure, by now, you've been forewarned by everyone." He grinned, revealing perfect teeth, tossing his head back to keep dark locks of hair from falling into his eyes. Eyes which were transfixed directly into mine. "Charles Gardensen."

I shook his hand, still not truly feeling the reality of the moment; I had imagined our meeting so many times, in so many different ways, but for some reason, not like this.

"I'm Brian Walden," I replied nervously, still shook up from his sudden presence. And then because that didn't seem to be enough, I added "Good to meet you." *God, why did I sound so stupid?* I was suddenly aware of how quiet it was in the room. Charles didn't seem to notice. Truthfully, I think he was sizing me up just as well. We released hands.

"Brian...a Celtic name. Interesting." He paused, indolently ambling towards a sleek black mini-fridge which I hadn't originally noticed near the front door. "You know, they aren't completely sure on what that name means." He knelt down and disappeared behind the fridge door only to return a moment later with a carton of orange juice. "Some historians claim that the name Brian is supposed to mean masculine, strong. Others claim it is supposed to mean noble, high." He scratched his chin. "See, I had a buddy back home - well, he wasn't really a buddy of mine...he was a cousin of a friend of a friend sort of thing..." he scratched his chin. "Honestly he was just kind of a fat louse who would come over and eat my food and drink my liquor." He placed his hands on his hips. "His name was Brian Antunes."

"Oh..." I said, not knowing what to make of his anecdote. Charles continued without waiting for a response.

"Anyway, he's the only other Brian I've ever known. And I didn't really like him."

I nodded, having no idea what to answer him with. I watched him, thinking at that moment how crazy it was that this was all really happening, here was Charles Gardensen, my roommate. Yesterday I sleeping in my closet-of-a- room on Stratton Street, reading about this guy and his family in the newspaper, and today here I am. Living with royalty itself.

"Oh, and just so you know, this is the 'Special Refrigerator'." He spoke from behind the fridge door, interrupting my thoughts.

"Special refrigerator?" I asked, having no idea what a 'special' refrigerator was. Was this something people talked about in high school? Was is like special brownies? *God I need to make some friends.*

"Yes, the Special Refrigerator." He opened the door to the mini-fridge wider so I could look inside. "Come take a look inside," he said, motioning for me to come closer. I immediately walked over towards Charles and the mini-fridge. "What do you see?" he asked, looking over at me.

I knelt over and peered inside. Water bottles, orange juice, apple juice, cranberry juice, pineapple juice, coca cola, and ice cubes filled the entirety of the fridge.

"Um, just soda, water and juice." I paused for a moment. "Are you diabetic?"

Charles laughed. "No, I'm not diabetic. I am somewhat of an alcoholic, though." he replied breezily.

"Oh..." I was at a loss for words. *Was he serious?*

"Anyway, nothing in the Special Refrigerator is what it seems. See, I've got a system going on in here." He pointed to the top shelf. "The water in these bottles is actually Vodka, the water in these bottles is rum," he continued pointing to the second shelf, "and down here are bottles of apple juice which are filled with whiskey, the coca cola is coca cola, the juice is all juice, except this one which is a cranberry cocktail mixer, and...the water in these bottles over here is actual water."

I stared at the fridge, not sure what to say. Looking at all of the liquor hidden in water bottles, I began to tense up. The campus violation policies were very strict at Princeton, especially with underage drinking. I couldn't afford to be kicked out of college and lose my scholarship because my roommate wanted to party. For a split second, and only that, I thought about saying something to Charles. I really almost did. And then I remembered, this *was* Charles Gardensen. His father practically financed the entire computer science department. He could probably torch the place without getting so much as a detention.

"Don't worry," he spoke up again, staring into my eyes, reading my mind. "The Special Refrigerator has never failed me. Not freshman year, not senior year, not when I had that stupid private tutor who got fired for stealing priceless family heirlooms, and not now."

There was such an air of certainty to his voice, I found myself starting to relax. "Oh, okay. It's just, I just, see I'm here on a schol -"

"In fact, the only reason I'm telling you about the Special Refrigerator," Charles went on, cutting me off, "is because I didn't tell the sixty-year-old maid who was cleaning my room one afternoon long ago, who got thirsty and decided to help herself to what she thought was a nice cold drink of water, but really was Grey Goose."

"I see. Wow."

"Yeah," he shook his head. "Anyway, she got really freaked out, sick, and vomited all over herself. It sucked."

"She was sixty?" I asked incredulously, feeling bad for the

poor woman already. Sixty and a house cleaner. I would be damned before I let such a fate befall my mother, or myself for that matter.

Charles squinted. "I think she was sixty. Maybe sixty-five. Anyhow, all I know is older people cannot hold their liquor." He shook his head. "Anyway, I would have been really screwed had it not been for my older brother. He gave that maid five hundred dollars to keep this knowledge of my hidden liquor from Astin, who specifically tells all the hired help to immediately inform him of anything rebellious like that. She took the money and never said a word. A month or so later she quit."

"Oh yeah?"

"Yeah," Charles closed the mini-fridge door and stood up. "She said we were the most miserable family she had ever met, and that she could not work in such a 'hostile' work environment, no matter how well we would pay her." Charles laughed, and then his face grew serious. "I think she was Catholic."

Having no idea what that was supposed to mean, I feigned a chuckle. While my mother and I weren't very religious, she always made sure I knew it was extremely important not to tread over anybody else's beliefs. "That was pretty nice of your brother."

Charles flinched for a split second. "Yeah. He was a good guy."

Was? "Oh...Oh, that's right," I said, feeling like an idiot, suddenly remembering the newspapers articles from a few years ago.

Charles glanced at his hands. "Yeah. He was the world's greatest older brother. The family favorite." He cleared his throat and looked up. "He was supposed to take over Astin's business, but...he died instead." He looked up at the ceiling. "Which was probably better, if you ask me." He added, softly.

I felt like such an ass for not remembering; I immediately tried to change the subject. "So," I asked, "how'd you end up here at Princeton?"

Charles stood there for a moment and didn't say anything. I thought I really pissed him off, but then he walked over to the sitting area. I watched as he grabbed a chair and stared at the ceiling for a few moments. I had no idea what he was doing. After a few seconds, he took a few steps forward and set the chair right underneath the smoke detector, which was now directly above him. With a feline gracefulness, he climbed onto the chair and stood on the stool, removing the smoke detector cap. He fiddled with a few wires, replaced the cap and hopped down. He sat on the chair and took out a cigarette. Lit it up. Inhaled. Exhaled. "My psychiatrist recommended the separation from home. He told Astin and my mother that," Charles suddenly slipped into a much deeper voice, "being in a stable environment with rules and authority and people my own age with goals would help influence a sense of responsibility in me. I could possibly discover a hidden talent or an academic subject that truly interests me, and will ultimately alter the course of my young and opportunistic life. "

Psychiatrist? "I see." I said, helping myself to the chair opposite of him. "Why Princeton?"

Charles took another long drag of the cigarette. "Elijah. He had planned on going to Princeton. He wanted to live in the dorms and study in the library and be just like everybody else."

I nodded. "Oh." I suddenly wished I had a cigarette in my

hand. Even though I had never smoked and particularly hated the way it smelled, it was something to fill the silences with.

"So," Charles rubbed the back of his neck. "Brian. What's your story?"

"Uh, it's not a very interesting one, I can tell you that much. No drunken sixty-year-old women or thieving tutors."

He smiled. "Amen."So..." he exhaled. "You're here on a full scholarship, huh?"

I must have looked surprised because he crossed his legs, trying to get comfortable and said, "Forgive me. I did a little homework. Or rather, Maestro Astin did."

I thought it was very in-character for Charles to refer to his dad by his first name. "He knows about me?"

Charles nodded, inhaling the cigarette for a moment. "He spoke to the Head of Admissions a few weeks ago, asking about my 'random' roommate" Charles rolled his eyes. "In case you can't tell, Astin is good friends with quite a few cheesedicks in administration here."

I nodded. It figured.

"He was impressed by your records. He liked that you worked your way from Stratton Street into this overpriced goddamned ivy league school." Charles paused and glanced at the walls of our dorm. "That spoke volumes to him. Reminded him that there is not excuse for my sorry ass lifestyle."

I nodded, partly glad that my indigent life was no secret anymore, and I wouldn't have to embarrassingly explain it in little ways and pieces. I should have expected the Gardensens to be able to access information about the person who was going to live with their son.

"Please don't tell me you spend time doing that." Charles said, cutting into my thoughts. He was pointing his cigarette over my right shoulder. I turned around to face a pile of Sudoku magazines I had brought from home.

I laughed. "Um, sometimes, it's a-"

"No, don't even try to explain those math games to me." He said back, with a smile. "Mathematics major?"

"Ah, pre-med, actually." I answered briskly.

"A doctor! Fantastic." Charles nodded, lifting his arms above his head and stretching languidly. "So I can bum prescription drugs off of you after graduation, right?"

I chuckled lightly. "Sure." I replied, even though the thought of illegally prescribing drugs terrified me to no avail and I sincerely hoped he was joking. Looking back on this, I'm pretty sure he was serious. "What are you studying?"

"I'm actually undecided at the moment. I was thinking of declaring myself an Art major at one point." Charles glanced at our walls. "In case you can't tell, I love paintings. I can't draw worth dick, though."

"Oh...I see."

"But the whole point of me being here is to dip my toes in the water, so to speak. I'm supposed to 'dabble in everything' and see what I like best." Charles stubbed his cigarette out.

"That sounds pretty cool."

"Yeah. It'd be nice to have a clue though. It scares me to say it out loud," he shrugged, "but I really just have no fucking clue as to what I'm supposed to do with my life. You know?"

I nodded, even though I rarely ever experienced those feelings. My entire life was pretty much a straight shot plan at that point. But even then, even in the earliest stages of our relationship, I wanted Charles to like me.

Charles folded his hands behind his head. "I took the

liberty of bringing a few items from my bedroom, I hope you don't mind."

I stared around the room, the entirety of it practically filled with his belongings.

Charles followed my glances, laughing. "Maybe I brought more than I should have, but oh well. I hope you don't mind all the same."

"Well, so long as there's room for my set of checkers, we're OK."

Charles grinned. "You're welcome to use anything I've brought in this room. What I've brought here is ours to share." Suddenly a phone started ringing. Charles reached into his pocket and pulled out one of those crazy phones I had seen walking by the electronic store, the ones where you could go online, check your email, listen to music and all that jazz. He peered into the phone and frowned. "You have got to be shitting me." He muttered under his breath. A second later he stood up. "So it's been good chatting with you. I have to take off for a little while, but I'll catch you later, huh?"

"Oh yeah, sure." I answered, nodding. He strode to the door, his oxfords clacking with each step. "It was nice to meet you." I called after him.

He took one look at me before shutting the door behind him and grinned briefly. "Likewise."

*   *   *

Ten minutes to midnight.

I had unpacked everything, (the scantiness of my belongings were only amplified by Charles assortment of black leather, crystal collectibles, spindly glass tables, and dark cherry wood) watched a delivery man drop off a few more boxes for Charles, organized my school books and supplies, and began going through the Princeton college planner. Hard as I tried, I couldn't fully concentrate on anything I was reading. My eyes wandered every few pages, over the walls, the paintings, over the room which I would spend my next few years in.

After a fruitless half hour of filling in the planner, I gave up. I phoned the only person I could. My mother. It was at times like this I really hated myself for not trying harder to make friends in high school. She answered on the third ring.

"Hello?"

"Hey M -"

"Brian!" She cried, immediately recognizing my voice, cutting me off before I could tell her it was me. "Honey! How's it going? Tell me everything!"

I let her know I had made it all right, found the place okay, and was already unpacked.

"That's wonderful! I'm so glad you made it there all right. That's absolutely great..." her voice trailed off. She remained quiet for a moment, just breathing onto the phone, excitedly, silently probing me about Charles.

"Yeah." I replied, playing the game, waiting for her to ask me about him first.

"What about your roommate? He settle in yet?" she asked, trying to sound nonchalant. I could hear the eagerness behind her words.

"You mean Charles Gardensen?" I asked innocently, as I began walking towards his desk.

"Yes, Brian. You can stop being an ass, now." My mother replied flatly, having given up on subtleties.

I laughed, standing in front of the desk, fiddling with the drawer knobs. I told her that Charles Gardensen was really actually quite nice. Extroverted, a bit direct, a little eccentric, but nonetheless pretty friendly. She was *thrilled.*

"Oh honey, that's *great!*" She squealed, loudly. I winced, holding the phone an inch further away from my ear. "Are you giving him his space?"

"Yes, mom, I am giving him his space."

"Oh good, good. Don't bother him too much, okay? And be nice, smile a lot. Be friendly. It'll be so nice if you two became good friends! You'd have so much fun together."

I groaned. "Mom, we're not girls. We don't just start instantaneously bonding with each other within the first five minutes of meeting." I rolled my eyes, suddenly surprised when one of the drawers, unlocked apparently, opened at my halfhearted tug.

"I know, I know, but…you know what I mean. You've spent your whole life in a book Bri, and so this will be good for you, I think. In fact, I'm sure it will be very good for you." She continued. Half-listening, I couldn't help but sneak a look inside the drawer. I knew it was despicable of me to do so, snooping around other people's possessions, and not just anybody's property either but *Charles Gardensen's property*, but I couldn't help it. My curiosity got the better of me. And so I glanced inside.

"Yeah mom, I know." I responded, awkwardly pulling the drawer a bit further out, and peeking inside. I don't know what I was expecting to find that day, but I certainly didn't expect to see what was actually inside there. A book. A simple, plain covered black book. It had to be at least three inches thick. I continued to ramble on, for my mother's sake. "Don't worry about it. Like I said, Charles is nice. I'm sure we'll get along fine." No, it wasn't a book. I plucked it slightly open, glancing over my shoulder first to make sure I was alone, and peered inside. Handwriting. Dates. It was a diary.

"Good, very good." she breathed out, cheerily. I wondered if she wanted me to break friends with Charles so badly because she knew I never really had any, or because she wanted me to be close to a Gardensen. Either way, I knew she meant well. And furthermore, I didn't have the balls to ask her.

"So, you're moved in. That's good. How do your things look? Not too shabby, right?"

I lifted the book out of the drawer and quietly began flipping the pages. I read words as they flew by. *Somewhere, in my mind…way in the back, behind all the screaming, shouting, breaking glass, endless games, toys, money, girls, meaningless one night stands, whispered words behind my back, solitude, emptiness, fights, cars, presents, outbursts – me just, absolutely fucking losing it-, behind the uncertainty of… myself…I try to believe… I'm innocent. I 'm innocent. I wasn't always like this. I was pure once. Just like you. I was pure.*

"Bri?" My mother's voice startled me back to life.

"Oh sorry," I replied, quietly shutting the diary and placing it back into the drawer. I was feeling pretty sleazy at that point.

"I asked how your things look, unpacked, and all." My mother repeated.

I glanced around the living room to see my pile of dog-eared books and sudoku magazines amidst Charles' entertainment center, complete with leather couching. While unpacking, I put up a school calendar on one of the few walls which wasn't covered with Charles' fancy paintings.

"Yeah, everything looks fine."

"How's your bed? I bought those sheets brand new at the

fabric store! Margie gave me a good discount, sweetheart she is."

My newly discounted thermal cotton bed sheets.

Charles 1,500 thread count Egyptian cotton sheets with Italian made linens. (Still in its package, unopened, tossed onto his bed as if an afterthought by one of his parents. Or a maid. Or a butler. Or the Sous chef.)

"Everything is great, mom. I'm really excited to be here. I miss you-"

"I miss you too, honey." She cut me off. "So much." I could practically see her squeezing the receiver to her ear, as if that would make me closer to her. It made me smile.

"Look I've got to go, it's pretty late and I've got to get up early tomorrow for Orientation."

"Okay, okay then, the old lady can take a hint. Call me soon. "

"Love you."

"Love you too."

We hung up. I drank a bottle of water out of the other mini-fridge Charles had brought in, which was stock full. He must have wiped out some super snack aisle or something, because we had all the best junk food stocked. Twinkies, cupcakes, hot pockets, Ben & Jerry's, you name it. Junk food, I would come to learn, was just one of his many childlike indulgences.

A couple of times I got daring and flipped the television back on. Back home, I was used to getting about five clear stations. All the newfangled channels on Charles' TV confused me; I had no idea what to watch. There were simply too many choices. After an hour of not being able to settle on any program, I gave up.

I walked around the room a few times, still trying to absorb the reality of what would be the next few years of my life. I fingered the spines of the thick heavy, leather-bound books lined on Charles' bookshelves. He had quite a few impressive titles up there, books I read in advanced literature classes, which I honestly didn't believe anyone could ever read for pleasure. I wondered if he truly enjoyed reading those titles, or if he had them up there just for show. You know, trying to live up to the image of eloquence that the Gardensen family portrayed in every appearance. To this day, I'll never know that answer.

Almost the entire evening, footsteps pounded by our door. I got a few phone calls where I would answer, and people would just breathe onto our line, and then begin laughing. A few times I even heard whispering outside the door. *This is his room. This is Charlie Gardensen's dorm. Are you serious? You think he's in there now? I dare you to knock! No way! Is he even in there? It's quiet, I don't think so. Come on, let's come back another time. It's late.*

I settled on the couch with a book and fell in and out of sleep over the next few hours. I would knock out every hour or so, and then stir back to consciousness along with the running footsteps past our doors, or some far-off music being blasted in another room. Just as my eyelids began getting heavy again, the door flung open. Light flooded the entire room. The crisp *clack clacks* of oxfords were heard against the floor. I opened one eye at the digital alarm clock.

1:53 A.M

"Listen to me" Charles' voice was loud, sloppy. "you have... to be...very...quiet. I have...a roommate." He flicked the light switch on. The black glow beneath my eyelids became orange. I shut them tighter.

"A roommate? Really? But I thought like...you were super rich. Why do you live...here? At the school?" A female voice. Also equally loud and sloppy. "And why do you have a roommate?" A giggle ensued. "Oh look, there he is! Sleeping on the couch!"

I could hear Charles stumbling, trying to kick both shoes off. A second later the lights were off again. "Hey, why'd you do that!? I can't see shit." she whined. More stumbling.

"I didn't know he was out here."

"Oh. Well, let's go to your place."

Charles laughed. "This *is* my place."

"Oh...right, right." A moment passed. "Why do you live on-campus again? Because I know a guy like you can -"

"I'm here... because... I made a promise to someone."

"A promise? To who?" Another tinkly laugh. Whoever she was, she had a beautiful voice. And she was incredibly wasted. They both were. The scent of cigarettes and alcohol began to permeate the room.

Charles sighed and for a moment there was silence. I could hear them both breathing deeply. Finally, Charles spoke. "No more questions. Okay?" He breathed heavily. Another few moments of quiet passed, and then footsteps. His bedroom door opened. More footsteps followed. A minute later the door was slammed shut.

I fell asleep wondering what she looked like, this mystery girl Charles had brought home on his first night at Princeton. I wondered if she was blonde or brunette. Tall and willowy, or short and curvy. I wondered if she was smart, like Carla Kissinger from my senior year calculus class. Man, brainy girls turned me on. I fell asleep wondering these things, thinking about girls, hoping I'd find a girlfriend before the year was up.

It never once crossed my mind how the presence of one particular girl would change both of our lives forever.

*   *   *

"You sleep okay last night?"

I had just woken up. The mouth-watering aroma of scrambled eggs and bacon twisted something inside of my stomach. I hadn't eaten in quite awhile.

Charles was seated on the coffee table, two feet away from me, smoking a cigarette. I sat up quickly, realizing I had fallen asleep on the couch and had stayed there the entire night. *Jesus. How long had he been there anyway?*

I wiped the sleep from my eyes and coughed. "What time is it?"

Charles glanced at his watch. "About ten-thirty. You're a heavy sleeper. I like that." He took a final drag of his cigarette and put it out right on the coffee table.

"Hey, don't do that." I said, slowly feeling more and more awake. "You'll ruin the table."

He stared at me blankly. "It's my table."

Feeling stupid, I paused before answering back, "Oh. Okay then." I looked him over. He was dressed in dark jeans, a white dress shirt with his sleeves rolled up at the elbows, and a black pull-over vest. His hair was styled with that disheveled-on-purpose look. I looked down at myself, still wearing yesterday's outfit. I felt like a slob.

Charles pointed to the dining room table. "Hungry?"

I looked over to where he was pointing and could have cried with happiness. The entire table was stockpiled with breakfast.

Plates of pancakes with butter and syrup, strawberries and cream, scrambled eggs and bacon, and a pitcher of orange juice decorated the tabletop.

Charles continued speaking as I stared, still not believing my luck. "I woke up hungry today, which is a surprise since I never really do, so I decided to do breakfast and do it right. Some girl I met last night recommended this place around here called the Yankee Doodle Tap Room." He laughed. "Anyway, I've heard good things. So please, help yourself." He motioned to the table.

"Really?" I asked, already making my way to the table. "This looks awesome." I sat down, thrilled at the prospect of eating a breakfast that wasn't instant oatmeal and picked up a fork rather quickly. I began piling pancakes on my plate. The smell of the food was even better up close, and my hunger was driving me crazy. "Thank you so much."

"Don't mention it," Charles replied, as I began devouring the wonderfully lavish meal, barely focusing on anything else. An explosion of flavor erupted in my mouth with the just first bite. I couldn't believe how good it was. I chewed, marveling at how enjoyable a simple eating experience could be. Charles walked over and took the seat across from me. He barely picked at his plate. Instead, he pulled out a another cigarette and lit it up. I noticed a 48 oz. bottle of water and two aspirin pills next to his plate of food and smiled.

"Party too hard?" I asked, in between bites of pancake, gesturing to the water and aspirin.

Grinning, he extended a bottle of maple flavored syrup towards me. "Hindsight, my friend, is a bitch." He eyed my plate. "Syrup?"

I took the bottle gratefully, heartily applying abundant squirts to each pancake. "Thank you."

Charles sat back in his seat. "Sorry if I was loud coming in last night. I'm not used to sharing such small living space, really."

I took another bite of pancakes. "Oh, no, it was fine last night." I lied. The food was so good, I felt so grateful. It was important to me to stay on his good side. I figured a tiny white lie was nothing. "You weren't loud at all."

Charles raised an eyebrow at me. "Really?"

I nodded, keeping my eyes on the plate. "Sure."

Eyes still on me, Charles bit into a strawberry. "You're a horrible liar."

I swallowed a piece of toast.

He laughed. "It's just, well… I'm really good at lying and so, it's easy for me to tell when others are lying."

I started laughing too. "I'm sorry. It's just; it was really no problem last night. I only woke up for a minute, but it's no big deal."

Charles smiled. "I'm glad you're not anal. We may just be able to get through this year without killing each other."

"Right…"

He leaned back in his seat. "I mean, Let's face it. I'm definitely not the most normal sort of roommate a guy could ask for. You'll probably get the crank calls, the stalkers, the gold-diggers, the thieves. My routine fights with Astin and my mother, sometimes the wonderful doctor." He lit up another cigarette. "If we're being honest here, I'm pretty much a fucking mess."

Doctor? I picked my fork back up. "Oh."

He held the cigarette between his fingers for a few

moments, before taking a drag. "And I'm moody. But I like to think all great people in history were moody and complicated. Nobody got famous by being fucking happy, huh?"

"I guess."

He nodded. "So what about you? Anything you'd like to bring to the table?" He knocked on the dark wood in front of him, smiling, for good measure.

I shrugged. "There's not a lot to tell with me, honestly." I looked down at my empty breakfast plate. Without saying anything, Charles placed the rest of the pancakes on my plate.

I looked up at him.

"Go for it. I don't like leftovers."

"Oh... okay then. Thanks."

Charles exhaled a cloud of smoke. "No problem. So... about you? Tell me about your family, since you know all about mine."

I folded my legs up underneath me, feeling nervous. "Well, um...I grew up on Stratton street, as you know. With my mom...my mom is a hair dresser. She works about sixty hours a week. My dad hasn't been in the picture since before I was born."

Charles raised his eyebrows. "Lucky."

I shrugged. "I guess. We've managed this far without him, so...Anyway, I wasn't really popular in school. I kept to myself a lot. Had my nose in a book the entire time, actually. We didn't really have money for distractions, anyway. So I just kept busy focusing on my future. Studying a lot. And...here I am. Full scholarship."

Charles whistled, clapping his hands. "Now how many

theaters do you think would have sold out tickets to *that* movie?"

I smiled. He had a point. My life did sound like some straight-to-DVD film you'd find way in the back of a video store.

"So I guess you are seriously overdue for a celebratory beginning-of-your-life drink?" Charles asked, finally putting his cigarette out. I was glad. Despite whatever he managed to do to disarm our smoke alarm that first day, I was still nervous every time he smoked inside the dorm. And still too shy to say anything to him about it.

"Um, I - I guess."

Charles regarded me for a moment. "Do you drink?"

I paused a moment, unsure how to tell him that no, I didn't drink. The main reason being that I had never drank before in my life, and didn't think it would be a good idea to start my first semester in Princeton.

"You do realize we can't be friends if you don't drink, right?" Charles asked, completely straight-faced.

I laughed nervously. "Um, I - I don't really drink a lot, is all..."

Charles narrowed his eyes at me.

"I guess what I'm trying to say is I've never drank before, ever...so...and now that we're in school, I-"

"Stop right there," Charles declared, cutting me off. "You've never drank before?"

I shook my head.

"And you're how old?"

"I never had a chance to. And if I did get a chance, I didn't have anybody to do it with. And if I did find somebody to do it with, I couldn't afford it." I admitted, slightly embarrassed. "Plus, I'm underage."

Charles laughed out loud. "I see. I see your point. Well, well, well. Tonight is your lucky night," he spoke with an air of resolution. "Because tonight, that chance is back. And trust me, you're going to want to take it."

I remember feeling torn between a fear of drinking for the first time, underage, illegally, with someone I barely knew, and the desire to make Charles like me.

"What are you doing tonight anyway?" he asked, cutting into my thoughts.

I shrugged. "I was going to go see what clubs are available to join in the student center, and probably walk around campus, familiarize myself with it more, you know."

Charles regarded this. "Okay, so basically you're not doing anything of importance." He clapped his hands. "We should explore town tonight. I know a few great places, you'll love them. And if you don't, well, I'll love them."

I laughed. "Um, okay, sure, I guess." I looked down at my empty plate and decided I was done with breakfast. "Okay," I glanced at my digital watch. "Well, I've gotta get ready"

Charles lit another cigarette. "Where are you going?"

"Orientation. At noon. I've got to be in the commons area."

He made a face. "Orientation? Come on, Brian, no one goes to orientation."

I smiled graciously, deciding to sidestep his comment. "Thank you for breakfast, Charles. It was the best meal I've eaten in...years. Honestly."

Charles raised his eyebrows. "The Yankee Doodle Tap?"

I nodded, wiping my mouth.

He shrugged. "Don't mention it. Anyway, meet me back here around ten. We'll probably take off a little after that."

My eyes grew wide. "At night?" I was used to being in bed by eleven.

Charles stared at me, half-smiling. "Um, yeah...ten at night."

I nodded. "Oh, okay then. Cool."

Charles stood up from the table. "I'm pretty impatient, so try not to be late."

Be late? Was he kidding? "Oh yeah, no problem. I'll be here."

"All right then, see you later." He grabbed his pack of cigarettes and tucked a loose one behind his ear. "I've got some running around to do myself." He waved, shutting the front door behind himself.

The night of my life, at ten tonight, I thought walking into the bathroom. I'd be lying if I said I wasn't excited. If my mother knew that her son and Charles Gardensen were going to hang out this very night I'm sure she would've been doing back flips.

I jumped in the shower, my mind stirring with thoughts. The scrawled sentences in his diary, how talkative he was, how detached he seemed from his family, his apparent fondness for going out on the town, drinking, smoking, how innocent he found me. Looking back on it, I should've picked up on these things and realized...realized how lonely he was.

Thinking about it now, this was the night that Charles would start shedding his first skins.

Chapter 4

Brian

"There she is."

I stopped in my tracks. "This is your car?"

Charles glanced up to meet my gaze, and then continued readjusting his sleeve cuffs. "That's the one."

"This car? Yours?" I asked again, our pace slowing down as we neared the magnificence parked at the end of the lot. I stood in front of it. A Porsche. Charles drove a *Porsche.*

The smooth electric blue exterior glowed in the moonlight. All black leather interior. Chrome rim tires. Tinted windows, of course, a requirement for any Gardensen. Polished to perfection, not a scratch on it. It looked like it had never even been driven before, like some miraculous force had just plopped it down there in the student parking lot. I stared at it, a mixture of exhilaration and shock filling my chest, my eyes. "How Why?"

Charles shrugged. "Are you really surprised that I drive a Porsche?"

Good point. I shrugged.

"It was my 'Happy Going away to College and Getting the Fuck out of My House' present from Astin." Charles informed me, "His frigid 'Pat on the Shoulder' and guilt came nicely tied along with it."

"Guilt?" I lightly scoffed, staring at my reflection in the tinted black, absolutely smudge-less windows. "My mother feels guilty, she gives me a hug, maybe a five dollar bill. Your father-"

"Astin." Charles cut me off, correcting me.

I continued, "Astin feels guilty, and you get a Porsche?"

Charles shrugged, reaching into his pocket. "You should see the car he drives for fun."

"I can only imagine."

"When he's not being driven around in his stupid Rolls, he toys around with his Bugatti Veyron."

"A *what?*"

"Bugatti Veyron."

Nothing came to mind. I had never heard of the model before. The only image I was able to conjure up was Charles' Porsche again, ten times shinier, with wings on the side, enabling the car with the ability to fly.

Charles put a cigarette in his mouth and in the process of lighting up explained the Bugatti Veyron. "It's one of the world's most exclusive sports cars. It *was* the world's fastest legal operating vehicle for a long time, until they made that new one...you know. Forget what it's called." Charles squinted and looked heavenward, as if trying to remember. He dropped his glance back at me. "Oh well. Anyway, it is now the world's *second* fastest legal operating vehicle ever produced. European." he added. "Astin would sooner shit his pants than drive or own an American car. He's quite the fastidious bastard, in case you haven't noticed."

"Right..." I responded, like I understood the quality difference between American and European cars. All I knew was last time I checked, a car wasn't a bus. I'd take any damn car available to fall into my lap. I ran my hand over the Porsche's cool blue exterior. "How much do, uh, Bugatti Veyron's go for these days?"

Charles languidly exhaled, blowing smoke upwards. "The particular model Astin drives clocked in just around one point three mil."

I stared at him as he finished exhaling. He tapped ashes onto the ground and nodded.   "Crazy bastard."

"Holy crap, man." He pulled a set of car keys from his pockets. "Frankly I think it's a present he bought himself to feel better about having a small *dong*."

I burst out laughing. "What?"

"I'm serious." Charles asked unlocking the car doors. "Napoleon complex."

I nodded. "Well, between you and me, I'd take a small dong for a million dollars."

Charles leaned back in his seat, pointing a finger at me. "Don't ever put a price tag on your dong, Brian. Especially not for something like money."

"Oh, right." I retorted, fastening my seatbelt. "Because having money is so overrated."

He offered a smile, but unlike his usual lopsided grin, this smile was not kind. A look of scorn quickly flickered over his face, there one moment, gone the next. If I had blinked, I would've missed it. And then a moment later he was himself again, sitting back up in his seat, turning the key in the ignition, bringing to car to life. "Circumstances, Brian. All about the circumstances."

*   *   *

True to my word, I had showed up to our room directly after orientation. True to Charles' word, only about a third of the people who were supposed to attend actually showed up.

Rounding off the stairs, I noticed a group of girls huddled a few feet away from our door. I could feel their heavily lined eyes following me as I walked past them, walked to the door, and then pulled out my room key.

One of them spoke. "Hey."

I looked up at her. She was, as I knew she would be, pretty enough to make me stop in my tracks.

I stared back at her, taking a moment to reply. "Hey."

She gave me a smile, parting full pink lips to reveal perfect white pearls for teeth."So, is like that your room?" A tall, lean brunette behind her asked. She was slowly rubbing her lower neck, dangerously close to her breasts.

I nodded, immediately flicking my eyes off her chest and onto the light fixture behind her. "Yep." *Jesus Christ, I just fucking said 'Yep.'*

"Cool." She replied, offering me a smile, slowly letting her slim arm dangle back down at her side.

"Yeah," I turned back to the door, not having any idea what to say. I opened the door a few inches and turned back around to face them. They continued to stare. I felt stupid as they just stood there, watching me. "Very cool." The third girl offered, another brunette, running a hand through her hair.

"Yeah..." I responded with my word of the day, apparently. I wished Charles was around. He would've known exactly what to say, how to effortlessly win them over or eschew them if he wanted to, invite them in for a drink, and keep them laughing or leave them standing in the hallway, wanting more. By the looks on the girls' faces, I could tell they were wishing they same thing.

"Well," the blonde walked towards me, taking slow deliberate steps. "We just wanted to let you and your roommate know," she paused, "that we live downstairs, so if you ever feel like hanging out sometime, give us a call." She handed me a napkin, containing 3 phone numbers, drawn in deep red lipstick. A kiss print decorated the bottom left corner of the napkin. At the sight of it, my pulse went up about 20 beats per minute.

"Okay?" She glanced into my eyes, her lips pressed together, curling upwards. The two brunettes behind her linked arms and also offered devilish smiles.

"Um, yeah. Sure. You got it. Th-thanks. Thank you." I looked past her, acknowledging the others behind her as well.

"No problem." She replied, accentuating her mouth with every pronunciation of the letter O. They stood there and watched me let myself into the room, waving as I went inside. I waved back shyly, and shut the door, relieved when I was inside.

I leaned against the door and shook my head. Up until that point in my life, no girl had ever given me her number before. Not only that, I had just gotten three phone numbers at the same time, from three extremely attractive girls. The blonde even initiated the conversation with me. Even though I knew their motivations must've been linked directly to the fact that Charles was my roommate, (in fact, I'm sure they were) I still was stunned by them. Flattered. *And where the hell are all the witnesses when something like this happens to me*, I thought sardonically, tossing the napkin onto an end table. I removed my knapsack and let it fall to the floor. Walking over to the refrigerator, I pulled out a carton of milk and poured myself a glass.

"What the fuck are you doing?!"

I gasped, the sudden realization that I was not alone hitting me hard. Flinching, I immediately lost grip of the glass. A satisfying shatter followed a second later. Milk and pieces of glass lay everywhere. I turned around to face a smiling Charles, arms crossed over his chest.

Open mouthed, not having even made that first sip, I stared at him.

Charles slipped his coat off and threw it onto a nearby couch. "It's almost ten O'clock Brian. Live a little." He raised his arms heavenward. "Have a..." he paused, theatrically bugging his eyes out. "A soda."

I shook my head and went to get a sponge from the sink. "Thanks a lot."

"Don't worry about the glass; I'll buy you another one." Charles grinned, obviously in a great mood.

In between wiping the mess up, I looked up at him and offered a smirk. "Actually, it was *your* glass."

"Oh." Charles shrugged, unaffected. "Then who gives a shit?" His cheeks were flushed from the cold weather outside. I stood up and threw the sponge in the sink. He clapped his hands, drawing back my attention. "No use in crying over spilt milk..." he looked at me waiting for a reaction and when I didn't give one he laughed at his own joke. "Okay, we I thought it was funny, but anyway," I smiled, washing my hands. "I'm taking us to The Red Room" Charles walked back into the living room area, cutting me off. "I'm sure you've heard of it, and I must say, I always do have a good time there."

The name flashed an image in my mind, a racy advertisement I had seen in the backs of magazines and newspapers. "I think so..."

"It's pretty hot and happening right now. Limited entrance, private booths, and they play pretty good music." Charles placed his hands in his pockets. "A little fancy schmancy, you know. They're uptight about the dress code."

I stood up. "I see."

"Do you have any special outfit for an occasion like such?"

"Uh," I looked down at myself, to the current outfit of my gray hooded sweater and jeans. "I can get some black slacks and, uh, maybe that plaid green button up shirt I was wearing the other day..." my eyes fell on the shirt, unfolded and wrinkled in the pile of clothes that needed to be washed.

Charles followed my eyes to the pile of wrinkled clothing and then looked back to me, with amusement in his eyes. "Right. Okay, follow me."

I wiped my hands on my jeans and followed Charles to his surprisingly normal-sized armoire. "What, no rotating closet?" I teased.

"The installation would've messed with the school's electrical wires." He replied, opening drawers.

I raised my eyebrows, unsure to laugh. "That's a joke, right?"

He didn't answer me. Charles continued rummaged through the contents of his drawers, messing through neatly folded articles of clothing, re-closing drawers, reopening them, tossing a few items onto the bed every so often. I caught sight of them through his quick movements. Chocolate brown slacks. A dark purple dress shirt. After a minute, he turned and faced me. Just then his cell phone began going off. He grabbed it and looked at it only to exhale in disgust a moment later. "Jesus Christ," he muttered under his breath. He opened the keyboard and began furiously typing, quickly sending out a text message and then shutting the keyboard back in place with a hard click. He then threw the cell phone against a wall. It hit with a hard *thunk* and landed on the floor. I stared at him wide-eyed.

"Anyway, where were we? Oh yeah, trust me; girls go completely ga-ga for this dress up shit. They love us in ties, they love our shirts tucked-in, hair slicked back, cologne, the works. They love all that shit." He placed an outfit in my hands and stared at my body. "Every single country I've been to, that's the one thing women have in common; they cannot resist staring down a sharp dressed man. Let me know how this fits. I'm pretty sure we're about the same size." He opened the bathroom door for me.

"All right." Arms full of clothing, I stepped into the bathroom. Charles flicked the light switch on and then shut the door behind me. I dropped the pile of clothing on top of the sink and took a moment to stare at myself in the mirror. To be honest, it felt strange to be trying on his clothing. We had only known each other for a couple of days; I was surprised Charles didn't mind sharing something so personal with me so soon.

Blowing a puff of air through my lips, I began assembling the decided outfit on. Slacks, undershirt, and dress shirt. Mid-arrangement, I spontaneously began pulling back the tags to read off the name brands of the clothing Charles had given me. I knew it was stupid and superficial, and I wasn't sure why I was doing it, but I just felt compelled to know what I was wearing and how much it was worth. Maybe a part of me was living vicariously through Charles for the night? Yeah, that and the fact that I had never truly worn anything much more worthy than twenty dollars at a time, probably. Either way, I wanted to know. They were, as I knew they would be, exclusive designer name brands, much akin to the merchandise advertised in windows of the stores I didn't dare step into.

I slipped the clothing on as carefully as possible, not wanting to be responsible for a ripped seam or anything, even though I was sure Charles wouldn't even notice, or care. I immersed myself in the quality of the materials, softness spreading over my entire body like nothing I had ever felt before. Charles was right; everything fit almost perfectly. I ran my hands up and down my torso, feeling silkiness against myself. I had never worn anything so posh or so well-fitted before. The clothes weren't two sizes too big, or a size too small, or worn, like they usually came to me. This time there was no air blowing through small holes in the fabric as I walked, no stains, no ripped seams. The length of the pants didn't drag a six inches past my soles. These clothes were perfectly pressed, precisely hemmed, well tapered, not a thread out of place.

I pulled the medicine cabinet open, my eyes falling momentarily on a few bottles of prescription pills, scanning it for hair gel. I grabbed a tube of something obviously belonging to Charles (it wasn't mine) and applied a liberal amount to my head. Unsure of how to style my hair, I defaulted to a slick-back motion I had seen in most movies. You know, one hand after the other, darting backwards into your scalp, like that. I had no idea what I was doing; I had never used gel before. After a minute of slick-backing I stood back and observed, satisfied with the finished product. *Not bad, not bad.* I stared at myself in the mirror, adorned in Charles' clothing with my newly styled hair, feeling...transformed. Seeing myself in Charles' clothing I realized I would've never been accepted into the club in my ancient black slacks and over-sized plaid shirt. I mean *plaid?* I always thought what my mother brought home for me to wear throughout my youth was decent. The clothing I wore growing up was always kept clean and kept me warm enough, wasn't that all that mattered with clothing? All the years I spent growing up dressed in little more than colorful cotton, I was blissfully ignorant. It was only then wearing Charles' clothes, I realized how poor my own apparel really was. How lowly it spoke of me, how easily it let others judge me. How much harder I had to work in other areas of my life to make up for a shoddy appearance. How much harder I would continue to have to prove myself. I bit my lip and ignored the feeling rising in my chest. Self pity never helped anyone.

"I said change your clothing, not shave your legs!" Charles voice gleefully boomed from the other side of the door, interrupting my thoughts.

"Very funny." I gave myself a final glance before unlocking the door and stepping out.

Charles eyed me up and down, a grin spreading across his face.

"Well?" I asked, placing my hands on my hips, a faux-model pose. "Am I passable?"

"My, my, my. Very well done." He put his hands on his hips, mirroring my stance   "Good." I retorted, smoothing down the front of the slacks, still not completely used to the material on my body. "Let's-"

"You need a jacket."

"A jacket?"

Without bothering to answer, Charles began leading the way back into his bedroom.

Instinctively, I followed him. With his back to me, Charles flipped through hangers, after few seconds of searching, he extended me a dark brown leather jacket. "That one's from France. Should bring you some good luck...maybe a ménage a tois?"

"Yeah, very nice." I laughed, taking it. I had to admit, Charles had impeccable dress taste. It was an extremely attractive jacket, simple in design, attractive in its dark brown color and in the style it was cut. The coat was made to give the impression of broad shoulders and a slim torso, tapered down the sides. I slipped it on, catching a whiff of the musky scent it emitted. It fit like a glove, and for the first time in my entire life I knew what it was like to want clothing for more than just shelter and protection. I remember never wanting to take that outfit off.

"Excellent." Charles gave a nod of approval, grabbing a black suede coat and pulling it over himself. His eyes lit up, as if suddenly remembering something important. "Last thing." He went inside his desk drawer and pulled out two pairs of sunglasses.

"It's ten o'clock, Charles."

He ignored my obvious remark. "Sometimes I've got to wear them, you know, so people don't recognize me everywhere. I don't want to get stopped 15 times and make up 15 different stories about how much I love Astin and his noble efforts to save the world before we get to my car, or the door, or wherever."

"You'll probably attract more attention wearing sunglasses at ten o'clock at night."

"Lots of idiots wear glasses at night." Charles extended his arm out to me, a pair in his hand. "What's two more?"

I took the sunglasses. *Giorgio Armani*, the label read. "I guess."

He slipped the glasses over his eyes "Ready?"

I slipped my pair on as well "Ready."

"How do you feel?"

"Honestly," I paused for a second, "like Cinderella."

Charles burst out laughing.

"Exactly like Cinderella."

CHAPTER 5

Brian

Sitting inside of Charles' car was an experience in itself. It was in that moment I was able to understand why car owners (let alone luxury car owners) looked at the bus with such disdain. In the car there were no strange odors wafting through the air, no sweaty crowds to push through. In the car you didn't have to spend the entire ride jerking back and forth over the bumpy streets, hoping that someone would get off at the next stop so you could actually get a seat. And then when you *did* get a seat, you usually ended up sitting next to someone fervently preaching about Jesus' second coming, or other. Not here. In the car, it was just me and Charles. I laid back into the passenger seat, the scent of cars' newness steadily infusing the air, filling my nostrils. It wasn't a scent I was accustomed to, but I decided I liked it.

Charles turned the key in the ignition. Needles flew up in the various odometers of the car, and a sharp beeping noise ensued.

"Seat-belts." Charles rolled his eyes. "Car will NOT let

you drive without them on, that noise will go on forever. I know - I've driven 100 miles without my belt on, with that thing continuously beeping."

"Well, safety first, Charles." I intoned, mock-chiding him. "You should know that."

"Safety my balls," he replied, adjusting the rearview mirror. "Any*hoo*," he tossed the sunglasses into an upper compartment in the vehicle. "She's nice right?"

I sighed. "I don't know, man. Compared to the public transportation system I've lived off, I don't know. Your car's all right."

Charles glanced at me, flicking the headlights on. "Your family doesn't own a car?"

I shook my head.

He shook his as well. "Shame. I'm sorry to hear it." He turned his head, reversing out of the parking lot.

I shrugged. "It's not that bad."

"I suppose if one's been conditioned that way, no."

I thought about that for a second, and then smiled. "Yeah, that means I'm screwed now, because I'm getting used to all of your nice shit around the place."

He laughed, throwing the gear into drive. "Indeed."

I had expected Charles to be somewhat of a reserved driver. All of his other movements, the way he spoke, examined things, smoked, ate, drank, walked, were carried out with a sort of feline gracefulness, each action carefully executed as if planned (except, of course, when he was completely smashed). In our short time together, I could already surmise that Charles Gardensen was the kind of person who took the time to enjoy things. A person who appreciated his surroundings, stretching out each experience as far as he could. With his given background and upbringing, time was not an issue. There were no ticking clocks in Charles' life. There were no admonishing hourglasses hanging over his head, whereas I could feel every hour I spent on entertainment or any sort of mindless distraction plague me, knowing I would never get that time back, cursing myself for not being more productive with it. Although I would later learn Charles definitely had his share of plaguing matters, time was not one of them.

Once out of the parking lot, we were at 60 miles an hour within seconds of driving. I grabbed hold of the armrest and glanced at him. "Charles, you're driving pretty fast, don't you think? We're still in the school zone..." Crosswalk signs everywhere forbade a speed limit over twenty-five.

He ignored me and stabbed a button on the dashboard. At once, music boomed through the front speakers, startling the hell out of me. I could feel the bass reverberating in my chest as we sped down the street. I glanced at the needle. We were at 65 miles an hour on a residential street. Looking back on it now, it's funny how at the time I'd rather have died being polite than squarely demand that he slow down the car. I gripped my arm-hold even tighter, keeping my eyes on the road, scanning it for pedestrians, or rabbits, or whatever creatures ran across the roads in the middle of the night in this town.

We passed four more streets, all of them becoming less residential and more urban. We zipped past a blur of bookstores, supermarkets, parks, and then a blur of all-night corner stores, bars, and dives. Groups of people stood in street corners, illuminated by lone street lamps, passing bottles around, laughing. They drunkenly clapped and whistled as we drove by, in admiration of Charles' car.

Charles turned the music down to where it was barely

audible after we passed them. "Fans are always nice. Drunk and high on crack-cocaine or not, they're always so uplifting, don't you think?" he asked, cheerily.

"Uh…sure" I replied, once again stymied by Charles unusual statement, unsure of how to reply, my ears ringing in the sudden quietness. He pressed a button on the driver side door, automatically descending his window. Lighting up a cigarette with one hand, and continuing to drive with the other, he glanced over at me. "Want one?" he asked, holding the pack out towards me.

"Uhhm," I thought for a second, keeping an eye out for the upcoming speed limit. "No, not really." Just as I wondered how to explain to Charles I had never smoked a cigarette before in my life, he spoke up.

"Don't tell me you've never smoked a cigarette before."

"I've never smoked a cigarette before."

He laughed. "Jesus, Brian. What are you, the Virgin Mary?"

I folded my arms across my chest. "Lung cancer is the most common cause of cancer-related death for men."

Charles took another puff. "Hey, Dr. Oncology, zip it and try one." He proffered another cigarette from the packet. "They make you look cooool," he raised his eyebrows, slowly exuding smoke from his nostrils.

I had to laugh at his ridiculousness. "Right." I adjusted myself in my seat, knowing I would make a fool of myself somehow trying to smoke it. "I don't really think I'd even like it, so…"

"You'll cough at first- everybody does."

"You know, it's a habit I really can't afford to acquire at this

time, being destitute and all, I'm afraid. Thank you, anyhow."
I replied with an apologetic smirk.

"Stop being a puss. Just try it." Charles continued holding
the pack out towards me until I gingerly slipped a single
cigarette out. Charles placed the carton back into his pocket.
He dug into his pocket and then passed me a Zippo lighter.

"Cool lighter." I commented, holding it to the car's
interior light to get a better look. The design was composed of
a simple black base color with the edges of the lighter outlined
in a lustrous deep silver. In the middle, also in fanciful silver
lettering, gleamed the unmistakable initials, C.G.

"Do you initial everything you own?" I asked, holding
the cigarette up to my face. I thought for a moment and then
sniffed it.

"Only the stuff I really like, therefore, it's less prone to
theft."

I shook my head. "Not if your thief is named, like, Carl
Green. Then it can be his initialed sterling silver lighter."

Charles gave me a flat stare. "Right, because there are so
many Carl Green's on this campus. Oh for God's sake, what
are you doing?"

"Nothing." I sniffed the cigarette one more time, and then
slowly placed it between my lips, moisture coating the filmy
paper. I knew right away I wouldn't like it.

Charles pressed another button, automatically turning
down my window as well.

"There you go." he nodded, encouragingly "Now inhale it.
And if you have to spit, do it out the window."

I nodded at him. "Here goes nothing."

What followed was the inevitable over-enthusiastic first
inhale, the thirty second coughing spell, and the semi-blurred

vision. I leaned out the window, expelling saliva, trying to get rid of the horrible acrid taste left in my mouth.

"So much for that." Charles laughed, pulling onto a main road. I could make out faint red neon lighting.

"Yeah, thanks anyway." I wiped my mouth. Charles finally slowed down, slowly treading down the street. Halfway down the block, we stopped.

"We're here!" He sing-songed, unfastening his seat belt. The beeping noise returned.

"Hail Mary full of grace, the Lord is with thee..." I recited, removing my seat belt as well.

We stepped out of the vehicle. As if one cue, a valet attendant approached us.

"Charlie! How are you tonight?" He extended an eager hand towards Charles. His name-tag read *Sergio*. Charles shook his hand, a million dollar smile playing his lips. "Very well, thank you Sergio."

"And you've brought a guest with you?"

"Yes, this is Brian Walden." Charles motioned me to Sergio.

"Very nice to meet you Mr. Walden, sir." He extended a hand to me; the excitement in his eyes seemed so real, I honestly couldn't tell if he was extremely good at his job or truly thrilled to meet me.

"Nice to meet you." I mumbled back, still tasting foulness, shaking his hand.

"Now Charlie," Sergio stepped forward, confidentially. "Take this to the doorman, he's a new guy, so don't forget to show it to him." Sergio handed Charles a set of V.I.P passes. "Here's your ticket stub for the car, you can hand it to any one of us down here and we'll bring it front immediately. Enjoy the night." Sergio gave us a half-bow.

"Yes we will, thank you, Sergio." Charles shook his hand, passing a hundred dollar bill into it. I tried not to stare at the money.

Hands in my pocket, I followed Charles past an entire line of clamoring, waiting people, which curved around the block. We stepped in front of the doorman, who gruffly acknowledged us. Charles produced the V.I.P passes and a fifty dollar bill. The doorman gave Charles a handshake, stamped both of our hands, and let us pass through the red rope. This was it.

We passed through the red doors, immersed in semi-darkness and energetic synthesized dance beats. Our only lighting came from low red overheads, and a mammoth disco ball in the center of the room. A mixture of smoke, perfume, and sweat wafted in the air, and my eyes nearly fell out of their sockets for the second time that night.

Here in the flesh lived out every fantasy girl I had seen between the pages of my old magazines. How poor of an excuse paper was for the real thing. These girls looked nothing like the cashiers or waitresses on Stratton Street, or anywhere in my neighborhood. Walking through the entrance, we passed by a lovely combination of waitresses, hostesses, baristas - all dressed to impress. They were tall, they were short, they were busty, they were tiny, they were curvy, they were slim; all of them beautiful, all different ethnicities, colors, shapes - this place had it all. I didn't even try to conceal my ogling; I simply stared at all of them, every single girl that managed to walk into my sight. They were all made up like movie stars, with rosy cheeks, wet lips, high cheekbones, tiny waists, perky breasts, long legs, long dark lashes, styled hair, glittering skin, and tanned bodies. I glanced at Charles, who seemed unaffected by their knockout appearances, walking right past them, stopping to offer a short smile or wink if they acknowledged him first. A few bartenders and security officers nodded at him, offering him handshakes. They all seemed to know him, waving, nodding, blowing kisses, smiling, welcoming him like a king coming home to his castle.

"Gardensen, good to see you." A man dressed in a suit, the size of a linebacker, pounded Charles on the shoulder.

If it hurt, Charles hid it well. "Avery, how's it going?" He shook Avery's hand.

"Same old, same old."

"Avery, I'd like you to meet a friend of mine. This is Brian Walden."

I stepped forward. "Nice to meet you, sir."

Avery and Charles glanced at each other and laughed.

"Sir," Avery repeated, wiping his forehead. "I like him."

"Yes, he's my latest protégé." Charles reached into his pocket and shook Avery's hand one last time, passing him a tip. "Take care, see you around."

"You got it, man."

We walked down the hall.

"Who was that?"

"Director of Security."

"No shit, that guy could've eat someone alive."

"Yes, he's pretty powerful." Charles reached for another cigarette. "I've seen some of his brute force in action, unfortunately. Nasty shit."

"Ok, like, what rules do I need to follow so I do not end up in that guy's way?" I asked nervously, following Charles down into the dance pit. People we brushed past stared at him, as if trying to recognize where they'd seen him before. He averted glances from people we passed. The dance number ended and Charles looked at me. "You're with me." A new song started up, the bass pounding throughout the entire room, pulsing in my chest. "No one can touch you."

"Charlie!" a stunning brunette wearing a glittering red dress called out in our direction. She walked over in quick rapid steps, her red heels clacking every step of the way. "How dare you come in and not say hi to me!" She scolded, her Hispanic accent surfacing just a bit. She walked over with her arms out, ready for a hug.

Charles embraced her. "Aura. How are you?"

"Good, baby. Good. Busy. Working. The usual. How are you? Who is this?" She nodded her head in my direction. I immediately took my eyes off the slit in her dress (which went from hip to heel) and forced myself to make eye contact with her. "Hi."

"Hello," she drawled saucily. She snaked an arm around Charles waist.

"Aura, I'd like you to meet Brian. Brian is my roommate at the University."

"Aiii, so you did it! You're in college now, huh?"

Charles nodded. "Good for you boy, damn. Good for you. You deserve a drink."

Again, Charles nodded. "Oh don't worry; there will be plenty of those tonight."

She giggled, before someone from the bar started calling out to her. She rolled her eyes. "Duty calls. Can't all be rich princes and princesses like this one, huh?" She teased, tussling Charles hair. He smiled at her. She leaned in close and whispered something in his ear. He smiled. She looked up at me."Nice to meet you, Brian."

"Nice to meet you too." I replied, catching myself staring at the slit in her dress again and then quickly averting my attention to a three hundred pound guy trying to buy a set of magnificent looking twins a drink. She gave us a carefree wave and disappeared into the throng of bodies by the bar.

*   *   *

"Are you ever going to try that drink?" Charles asked, bringing my attention back to our table.

I looked down at the frosted glass placed in front of me.

"You won't die, I promise."

"I know." I continued starting at it, encircling the glass with a hesitant palm. Charles had ordered something called a Hairy Navel for himself, and requested a Fuzzy Navel for me, explaining to the waitress that I wasn't ready for the jump yet. She laughed, never checked his I.D, (in fact, even though we were obviously underage, nobody bothered us for identification) and brought us complimentary cigars. A few years later, I ran into a gentleman selling those same cigars. They were worth about $25 dollars apiece.

Charles exhaled a cloud of smoke, and unlike the cigarette smoke, this smoke was thicker, much spicier. It lingered in the air much longer. "It's a highball. Don't worry."

"A what?"

"Highball. Low concentration alcohol, high concentration non-alcoholic mixer. Safe starter drink." Charles nodded reassuringly.

"You really are an alcoholic, aren't you?" I asked incredulously. He burst out laughing and I smiled, pleased at my newly found dormant social skills.

I lifted the glass to my lips and took a sip. Charles watched intently, as I downed a rather large gulp of my first alcoholic beverage ever. I wiped my mouth, tasting subtle bitterness underneath the sweet juice. The sip itself wasn't so bad, but the strangely bittersweet aftertaste was what got me. I don't know what I expected; I had never drank alcohol before. Visions of myself air-humping and then puking on random girls on the dance floor floored my mind. I sat quietly for a moment, letting the first sip settle in.

"Sooo…" Charles raised his eyebrows.

I licked my lips. "It's okay. A little tart." I took another sip, paused, and then another. "If I sip it fast, I don't taste the bitterness so much." Charles laughed. "A Fuzzy Navel is probably one of the sweeter alcoholic drinks out there."

"Oh…"

"Don't worry, just work on that one and as we work our way up the ladder, they'll taste better and better. Trust me." He raised his glass to mine. "Cheers." We clinked glasses, both downing another sip.

Charles and I sat in our V.I.P booth, our waitress popping by every few songs, refilling our drinks every single round and emptying out Charles' ashtray.

"Two screwdrivers, please." Charles addressed the waitress, the second time she came round to our table. I brought the glass to my nose, sniffed, and downed it, swallowing it as quickly as possible, trying not to taste the vodka running down my throat. A moment later I felt a quick trail of warmth rush down my chest, settling in my stomach. It was the strangest feeling.

We sat there, "absorbing the goodness", as Charles called it. Half an hour went by, and after awhile I could feel him watching me. "Another one, then?" He asked eagerly, tapping his cigar to the ashtray, obviously pleased at my enthusiastic response. Though I wasn't too crazy about how liquor tasted, I guess it was the very fact that I, Brian Walden from Stratton Street, was sitting in a V.I.P booth at the hottest club in town, next to one of the wealthiest people in our state, watching a beautiful girl in a cage dance for my very viewing pleasure, which made me feel as if tonight was no ordinary night. Any other night I would be at home, studying, watching T.V, eating noodles, daydreaming, with a book under my arm. Not tonight. Who knew when another chance like this would come around?

"Yeah, actually. Another one sounds good." I agreed, still trying to guess if at that very moment or not I was drunk or not. To be honest, I felt pretty much the same. Just looser. And definitely warmer. *This shirt collar is too tight,* I thought, tugging at it. I unbuttoned the top two buttons and leaned back in the seat. Our waitress reappeared, emptying Charles ashes into her tray.

"Another drink, sir?" She asked, flashing him an alluring smile

Charles looked heavenward. "Ahhhh…." He scratched his chin. "Let's do…Cape Cods. Two Cape Cods, please"

"But of course." With a small bow, she descended into the bar area.

" I'm not gonna get sick tonight, right?" I asked, toying with the little red straw in my empty glass, suddenly having visions of myself vomiting all over the place. "Like, I don't want…that."

"Relax, Brian, I've got you covered. As long as you don't

mix your liquor, you should be okay. We'll stay in the vodka *familiglia* for now."

I nodded, glad that he knew what he was doing. I had no idea what was in any of the drinks he was ordering, had no idea what the hell a Fuzzy Navel, or a Screwdriver, a Kamikaze, or a Cape Cod entailed. I also began to wonder who came up with such odd names for drinks. In the next few hours I would learn that there were even worse names for drinks.

We sat together watching the crowd, watching the cage dancer erotically entangle herself against the bars, sometimes glancing at each other, laughing at a particularly bad dance move being made by some idiot out on the floor. For a long time Charles and I sat there, not speaking, simply observing. Funnily enough, the silence between us was not an uncomfortable one. I found it quite relaxing, actually. I felt that there was more communication in our sideways glances and hidden smirks than there would be if we were actually engaged in conversation. It was easy, sitting there together, Charles smoking and nodding his head to the rhythm of each song, me tapping my foot and watching everybody dance, dance, sipping my drink, dance, imagining myself out there, finishing my drink, dancing with everybody else. The song faded out, and a bouncer strode by our booth, announcing a break for the redhead in the cage. He glanced at Charles, recognizing him, and then rushing over to our table.

"Mr. Gardensen, how you doing tonight? Everything okay?" He reached over, energetically shaking Charles hand.

"Everything's fantastic, thanks. I'm having a good time." Charles fluidly slipped a cigar out of the open box and held it out to the bouncer. "You must have one on me. They're exceptional. I insist."

The bouncer shook his head in refusal. "Very generous of you, but I apologize, I must pass."

"I absolutely insist. You must have one." Charles repeated, stubbornly holding the cigar out. Out of politeness, I'm sure, the bouncer took the cigar in his hand. He held it close up to his face, examining it, and whistled. "Are you sure?"

"Positive."Charles nodded. "Enjoy."

"Thank you." The bouncer stepped closer to Charles and leaned in confidentially. "If you need anything special at all tonight, you let me know, okay?"

Charles nodded again. "I'll keep that in mind."

The bouncer nodded briskly, then turned to me and vigorously shook my hand as well. "Any friend of Charlie's is a friend of mine."

I smiled at the bouncer, unable to think of anything to say. He gave us a quick bow and strode off, hastily talking into an earpiece. The song ended and the cage dancer jumped out of her cage, momentarily standing in front of our booth. Standing, she smiled at both of us, her face flushed.

"Wasn't she something tonight, Brian?" Charles asked stridently, for the benefit of the dancer, reaching into his pocket, indubitably searching for his wad of gargantuan bills.

I nodded, smiling. For some reason I couldn't seem to stop smiling. I stared at her flushed skin, no longer embarrassed by it, feeling incredibly relaxed. "Yeah, she was pretty cool." I said to the dancer, hoping she'd turn around so I could check out the rest of her one last time before she disappeared in the abyss of bodies. She smiled, and I had never seen anyone smile so beautifully. Charles lifted a hundred dollar bill out of his wallet and stuck it in his mouth. I had no idea what he was doing, but the dancer knew exactly what to do. Keeping that smile on her face, she slowly walked over and straddled Charles. He leaned back in his seat as she began running her hands up and down his body, and I mean *all over*. Without any warning, she leaned in close to his face and extracted the money from his mouth with her own. She turned to me and winked. I watched in amazement as she stood up, smiled, and walked away.

"Whoa...whoa," I said as Charles began lighting up a cigarette. "I think she likes you." Charles laughed, fiddling with the straw in his drink glass. "Cage dancing doesn't seem like a real lucrative form of income."

"Hey, *I* would dance in that black thong and whip my head around wildly if it would get me money like that." I proclaimed, slamming the empty glass down.

Charles laughed. I glanced back at the dance floor, laughter bubbling in my throat, about to point out a horrendously bad dancer, a guy who was simultaneously air-humping and snapping his fingers over his head when I noticed Charles was staring at something over my head. He quickly made eye contact with me and then glanced back past my shoulder, his eyes filled with gameness.

I turned over to see two petite looking girls standing near our booth. Their slender arms, bejeweled in bangles, were drawn to their sides, purses tightly clutched in their small hands. Their good looks were equally stunning, both girls decked out in practically painted-on strapless dresses, (one yellow, one blue) revealing bare shoulders, bare backs, and bare legs. I looked them up and down, not realizing how pointedly I was really staring at them until my gaze reached their faces and found them staring back at me. They offered us half-smiles, their pretty eyes fluttering from Charles, to me, back to

Charles again, as if unsure which one of us to look at. I glanced back at them, and then turned back to Charles.

Still smoking, Charles slowly exhaled a puff of the cigar and stared at them, as if challenging one of them to speak. I looked back at the girls. They remained silent, the brunette in the yellow dress twirling a lock of her hair, slightly rocking side to side, in rhythm with the music.

I glanced back at Charles.

He continued smoking and staring, taking no note of the silent questions I was sending him with my eyes, a slight smile playing his lips.

I turned back to the girls. The blonde in the blue dress bit her lip, twirling a lock of her long, golden hair, eyes burning holes into our booth, our empty drink glasses, our opened box of cigars, and the fifty dollar bill Charles had left on the table as a tip for the waitress. Charles lifted a leg and crossed it over his knee, eyes still on the blonde in the blue dress.

As hard as the she tried, the blonde couldn't get Charles to say a word. She probably wasn't used to approaching guys. She was probably surprised that we hadn't offered her a drink yet, or acknowledged her with much more than a stare. As if breaking a secret rule for extremely good-looking girls, she hesitated, and finally spoke first. "Hi." She smiled at Charles, her teeth slowly peeking out underneath glossy sensual lips.

"Hello." Charles raised his head, acknowledging them. Feeling very loosened up myself, I lifted my hand in a semi-wave. *Look at me, interacting with girls*, I mused.

"Is that seat next to you taken?" The blonde pressed, coyly cocking her head to one side.

"This seat?" Charles asked, steadily placing a palm on the empty red velvet space to his left. Her eyes followed his unhurried hand movement the entire time. She nodded, biting her lip.

Charles grinned. "Yes, actually, this seat is free. And so is the one next to my friend right there." Charles pointed to the empty space right next to me. I stared at the empty space next to me, suddenly aware of how much room we really had left in this booth.

The two girls grinned at each other, as they made their way behind the table. "Perfect." The blonde announced, moseying over to Charles side of the couch, traces of sweet perfume trailing the air behind her, as she sat herself down. "Absolutely perfect."

CHAPTER 6

Charles

I tossed the empty bottle of vodka into the ocean, waiting for the sound of its splash. I closed my eyes. Waited for it. "I think it was the Tiger."

He raised his eyebrows at me, walking over, grabbing onto the ledge for stability. "Really? Really, Gardensen? The tiger?"

I nodded coolly, taking a drag of from my cigarette. "Don't tell me you're one of those…" I squeezed an eyelid shut, trying to conjure up the right word, not quite finding it, "…people…"

He laughed before I could finish my sentence.

We were both pretty smashed. It was Friday night and I had invited Brian to a club, and then we crashed an after-hours party, stole a bottle of vodka, walked into a gas station and bought a bottle of cranberry juice. We had spent the better part of the last hour taking turns chasing sips of vodka with the juice. Thereafter I decided it was time for Brian to learn how to drive a stick shift. The test car? My Porsche.

"I dunno man, this is wrong in so many ways," he slurred

after I had finally convinced him to get in the driver seat. He clipped his seatbelt on. "Soooo many ways…"

I slid in beside him, fastening my seatbelt. "Look, s'harmless. We're not even… on a main road. *Nobody* drives on this road."

"Astin Gardensen's son drives on this road, apparently!" He exclaimed, poking me my ribs forcefully.

"Ow, look, whatever, it's fine, it's totally fine. You just gotta take this all the way down… and then the lake will be there. Easy. Easy peasy lemon…fuckhole."

"Okay, okay, okay. I'm convinced." He laughed, fumbling to stick the key in the ignition. "But if we die, or kill someone, or get arrested, I'm telling them it was all your idea. You made me do it. This is entirely your fault."   I threw my hands up in the air. "Done deal." Rolling down the window I continued."It wouldn't be the first time it's happened, either. You know, the year my brother died, I drove his Lexus straight into the wrought-iron gates in front of our house. The goal was to hurt myself, which worked real well that night. Astin was so pissed. The car was totaled and he had to have someone redo our gates. I fractured my right arm, and two ribs, but he didn't give a shit about that."   He paused to look at me.

"Did that really happen?"

I pointed to the clutch. "Yeah. It sucked, man. Learning to jerk off with the other hand, not so fun."

Brian stared at me for about twenty long silent seconds before speaking. "I don't have a driver's license."

I chose to ignore this. "Okay, you're gonna wanna put your foot on the clutch. No- that's the brake, the left one, the lefter one. The clutch. Okay, good. Push it all the way in."

"Okay…"

"Okay, now start the car."

He turned the key in the ignition. Nothing.

"Your foot's not all the way on the clutch, man. Push it all the way in."

"I am."

"No you're not. More. More. Okay, go ahead."

The Porsche started up.

"Success!" he cried, clapping his hands.

I nodded encouragingly, "Ok, put it into first. Up left. Okay, good, now slowly accelerate…good…"

"Do I put it into second gear now?" He reached to shift and I pushed his hand back. "Wait, wait until you hear the revving get louder, that's when you want to change gears, like now…now, now now! Now!"

The car stalled.

After a few more minutes of Brian laughing, unnecessarily shifting gears at the wrong times, stalling the car, and me screaming directions at him, I ended up driving us both to the bridge.

"Now why's it when you change gears, it's so smooth. But when I do, the car gets all…bumpy."

"Because I'm shifting gears at the right time, dumbass. And because you have to clutch when you shift gears. You can't just shift the stick anytime."

"Mmm." He laid back in his seat and smiled. "I don't know if you know this, but your car is *super nice*, man."

I smiled briefly. "Thank you, Brian."

"Like, I wish I had a car like this. You must get so many girls taking their…panties off, for this car." He sighed. "So lucky. I want a girl with her panties off."

I laughed. "All in good time, my friend. All in good time."

A couple of hazy minutes later, we reached the end of the Sherman road. I parked the car and we walked began walking towards the woods, breathing the cool night air deeply. It felt good. I looked over at Brian who was taking huge, ridiculous breaths of air and after a minute of watching him, I had to ask. "What the hell are you doing?"

Brian inhaled deeply, and exhaled. "I'm respirating!" He took another deep breath and let it out. "Sixty-five percent of alcohol leaves the body from respiration. Did you know that? I bet you did not. I learned that when I was thirteen years old. I did a project on the effects of alcohol on the human body. I got an A plus *plus* on that thing!"

I shook my head. "Fantastic."

"Yeah. It rocked."

I laughed as we continued getting closer and closer to the lake that was hidden behind the all the trees and shrubbery. It was a smaller lake, perfect for a couple of people who wanted to get away from the rest of the world for a little while. We were almost there.

In the middle of our walk, my cell phone began to go off. I grabbed it instantly shutting the ringer off. I didn't want Brian to hear my phone going off. I glanced at him; he was playing the air guitar behind me, stumbling along. I looked down at the caller and sure enough, it was her. Goddamnit. Goddamnit.

I closed my eyes, gritting my teeth.

Not now. Not. Now.

*　　*　　*

"Ever hear the story of the Lady or the Tiger?"

He shook his head.

"Well," I took out a cigarette, and began lighting it, "it was my favorite story growing up. My favorite story ever." I smiled, a little embarrassed, not having told anybody else this about myself. "Elijah's too."

He gave me a tipsy smile, still half-drunk. "What's it about?"

I took another drag of my cigarette and wondered how to tell the story, when before I knew it, I was already speaking.

"Well, you see, there's this beautiful, rich, princess, right? And she's completely gorgeous, and everybody respects her and her family, and for the most part, she's a decent person. Except…she has this horrible flaw." I paused to take another drag. Brian stared at me expectantly.

"She has this…raging jealousy problem. Everyone in the kingdom knows about it, she was born that way. Whenever she can't something, or she feels that she doesn't have enough love or attention from her family and friends, she rages. She destroys things, hurts people, hurts herself. She has beautiful tan skin, full red lips, long dark hair, and green, green eyes. Envious eyes. Hungry eyes. Eyes always looking for more, eyes always reaching for what they can't have."

"Anyhow, she meets a boy one day. This boy is a hard worker, honest, handsome, respectful, and floods her with all the love and attention she desires. Of course, he's extremely poor, and is a laborer, someone she could never marry. You know how that goes. Anyway, they carry on a secret relationship for months, before the princess's father finds out."

"There's only one person the princess has a hard time standing up to, and it's her father. He is the ruler of the land, after all. When he finds out of their secret courtship, he goes insane at first, ordering a public execution for the young boy she's fallen in love with. But she talks him out of it. She begs, pleads, threatens to kill herself, cut off all her beautiful hair, and run away."

"The king, distressed at the seriousness in daughter's threats, decides that he will alter the punishment for the boy. Instead of definite public execution, he decides to give the boy a chance for life. The king summons the boy up before him. He explains that the next morning, the boy will be led into a room. Inside the room will be two doors and two doors only. One of the doors will be a way out, a way out of death and a chance for life. The other door, unfortunately, will lead him to his demise."

"How?"

"Well, it's quite simple, really." I admitted, taking another drag. "Behind one door lies a beautiful, kindhearted, young lady, one of the king's loyal servants. If the boy chooses the door with the lady, they will be married and released to be free that very day; their marriage ensuring a solid end to the boy's relationship with the princess."

"And behind the other door lies one of the king's tigers, one that's been purposely starved for weeks, trained to kill intruders and the like."

"The boy is terrified, listening to the king. After the king explains the procedure, he leaves the room where the boy is being held captive. He lets the princess in to say goodbye to her lover. She waits until they are alone, and begins speaking quietly to her lover. She whispers to him that she will be there tomorrow; she will be in the crowd, watching him, when his time comes to choose a door. She tells him that she is going to find out which door holds the beautiful woman beforehand,

and she will signal to him which door it is. She says one blink of her eyes means Door 1, and two blinks mean Door 2."

"The boy is so relieved by her good heart that he weeps, he holds her and weeps, telling her how much he loves her, and thanks her over and over again for promising to save his life. They kiss their last kiss, and she leaves him in solitude while he awaits his fate the next day."

"The next day arrives, and the boy is summoned to the room which holds his fate. The king and most of the royal family, guards, and servants are watching through a window, watching, and waiting. The boy stares at the doors, one to his left, one to his right, both exactly identical, both giving no signs whatsoever of any difference, both dangerously awaiting him.""He swallows hard, and glances over to the princess, who is also silently watching him behind the window. She wears a silk scarf over her face, but leaves her eyes uncovered. He stares into her eyes, waiting for an answer, waiting. She glances at him, and blinks twice. He stares at the second door, and back at her, and she blinks twice again.""Before he can choose the second door, he stares at her for a moment and realizes her beautiful green eyes, her eyes that he's been so deeply in love with, are flashing. Flashing so green, he's never seen them so green. He pauses, and starts to think. He knows of her horrible jealousy, her fits, her tantrums, he's seen them firsthand himself. He knows of the malice that can rule her heart. He glances at her eyes again, flashing brilliantly. With what? With jealousy? With fear? With anger? Could she truly do this to him? It hadn't crossed his mind the night before, but he realizes, she could easily be sending him to the Tiger. Her infamously jealous heart would just as easily rather watch her beloved die, than see him find love and happiness with another beautiful woman. Was the rage truly that strong? Would she really rather watch him die? For a moment he is thrown, unsure of his ability to trust her selfish heart. Seconds feel like hours, and the boy knows he is running out of time. He says a prayer, holds his breath, and decides to believe in the promise the princess gave him the night before. He decides to believe in their love. And so with the most tentative, fearful steps he's ever taken in his life, he closes his eyes, and places his hand on the doorknob of door number two. Takes a breath. And without a second more of hesitation, pulls the door all the way open, awaiting the answers."

Brian blinked, holding the ledge of the bridge, leaning semi-dangerously over. "*And?*"

I put my cigarette out on the cement. "And nothing."

"What do you mean '*And nothing?*' What happens?"

I shrugged. "That's the point, Brian. That's how it ends. You have to make up the ending. In the end, was it the Lady, or the Tiger?" I didn't say anything for a minute, letting silence soak in between us. Out of pure habit, I plucked another cigarette from my pack and lit it up. "I suppose that's one of the reasons Walt Disney never picked the story up."

He laughed. "Yeah."

"So what do you think?"

"About…"

I rolled my eyes. "The ending, dumbass."

"You mean, which fate he ended up getting?"

"Yeah."

He was quiet for a moment. We stood in silence, for a moment, watching the city behind the bridge. Then he spoke. "The Lady. I think she gave him to the Lady." He let go of the ledge and steps down onto the ground. "I don't think there's any real way you can…kill someone you love, like that, you know?" He looked at me, still half-slurring. "I mean, yeah, she was an insanely jealous bitch, but somewhere down there, if she *really* loved him, she would want him to live. She would want him alive, she would want his happiness, even if it cost her own. She loved him." He paused, crossing his arms over his chest. If we weren't so drunk, we'd probably be freezing our asses off. "So yeah, I think it was a happy ending. I think she gave him to the Lady."

I offered a half smile at his optimism, taking a rather long drag of what felt like my sixtieth cigarette of the night. *I've really got to stop smoking.* I caught Brian watching me and had a feeling he was thinking the same thing. I smiled at him. "What?"

"Nothing." I cocked my head to the side and shrug. "Nothing." I took another drag of the cigarette. It didn't taste so good."It's just, it's funny."

"What's funny?""Your answer, it's funny." I cleared my throat. "See, that's exactly what Elijah believed." I pointed my cigarette at him. "He always believed she gave her lover away to the Lady." The cigarette really wasn't good. It had gone stale. I threw it into the lake.

"So, what ending do you believe in?"

The smile disappeared from my face. "It's obvious." He remained quiet, watching me. "Of course she gave him the Tiger. Jealousy isn't a little red balloon that floats in and out of your sky every now and then. It's a personality trait. It's a natural instinct." I shoved hands into the pockets of my coat. "If you love someone so much, and you can't have them, what makes you believe anyone else should?"

CHAPTER 7

Brian

Friday we went out for drinks. Saturday was spent at another club. Sunday we bowled and caught a jazz concert. Charles, a very skilled bowler and naturally good at sports, nailed a score of 210. I was right behind with a score of 69. On Monday, Charles gave me two hundred dollars to complete all of his homework assignments for him. I finished them in 3 hours, and mailed a hundred dollars to my mother. Afterwards, we went to a dorm party. Tuesday we had dinner with three girls Charles met at the park earlier that day. I ended up making out with one of them while the other two disappeared with Charles. By Wednesday, I was spent. I was averaging about four to five hours of sleep a night, hanging out with Charles and completing all of my assignments and going to all of my classes. Charles on the other hand, slept in every day and only attended a handful of his classes every so often. Even so, this didn't stop him from approaching me Wednesday night.

"Time to put the books awaaaaay..." he sing-songed walking over to the desk I was studying at. Textbooks and papers were strewn everywhere. I was reviewing for an exam that night and was just about to hit the library.

"I can't Charles, I wish I could." I told him. And it was the truth.

"What do you mean you can't?" He asked, propping himself up on the desk next to me, popping a stick of gum into his mouth. He offered me a piece. I shook my head. "Let's jump in the Porsche. I want to buy a few new CD's. We could hit up the mall. I'll buy you a bag of candy from Sweet Factory..." he joked.

"I've been neglecting my studies enough as it is."

He made a face. "You've been neglecting losing your virginity enough as it is."

I buried my head in my hands. "You're probably right, but still...I can't mess around with my scholarship." He began going through the loose papers on my desk, mussing through them. "I have to go the library in a few minutes anyway. I'll probably be there all night."

Charles shrugged. "All right. I never ask twice." He grabbed his coat and strolled out the door a minute later. After he left, I sighed and told myself I made the right decision. No matter how badly I wanted to go with him, no matter how dumb people would consider me for turning him down, I told myself I made the right decision.

*　　*　　*

Truth be told, I loved college. Charles and I were having a lot of fun together. I loved my classes, loved that people recognized me, loved that it was easier for me to make friends. In the blink of an eye, I had gone from being a nobody to being somebody. It was amazing. And I know I owed that all to Charles.

For awhile, anyway.

I remember this one time, Charles and I were out and we met these two girls for dinner. The restaurant manager seated us first even though we had no reservations and there were people waiting in line in front of us. The staff seated us in the center of the room. We walked past the other tables, soft music playing, people stopping their meals mid-bite to glance at us, candles being lit at our table hurriedly by waiters. Before we had even ordered a complimentary bottle of wine was sent over to our table. Plate after plate of breads, sauces, pastas, and steaks were periodically dropped off at our table, our wine glasses never empty, our I.D's never once asked for. Throughout the entire meal Charles kept us laughing, entertaining us with stories so damn ridiculous, they had to be made up. In between bites of the meal, Charles offered the extra cigars to nearby patrons, workers at the restaurant, anybody, everybody. We sat there for two hours, loudly laughing and speaking. No one complained, or protested to our noisiness. Most people stared at us, with this look...only now I think I can say what they truly felt for us was not contempt, or exasperation at our recklessness... but envy. They were jealous. How young and handsome and powerful Charles was that moment, banging his fists on the table, ordering wild amounts of sumptuous food, not giving a damn about the costs, the time, or the people around us.   I know for a fact, if I never met Charles, I would probably never experience such treatment in an entire lifetime. People running around, free this, free that, complimentary this, exclusive doors opening without so much as a second thought. It was a dream life. For awhile, anyway.

*   *   *

We had just left a party in the fancier part of the suburbs. It was a friend of a friend's place, and being Charles he naturally just crashed it and invited me along. Charles surprisingly hadn't been recognized yet. We were sitting in the master bedroom of the owner's home. Charles loved doing this at every party, going upstairs into the master bedroom of the home and going through the owner's stuff. This habit of his freaked me out to no end, because I was so terrified of getting caught, thinking the owners, or anybody really, would walk in and catch us in there at any moment. When I mentioned this to Charles he merely shrugged.

"Who would believe that I would need to steal anything from anybody? I'll just act drunk and pretend to be looking for the bathroom." He had done this in front of me, a couple of times. He liked going through the drawers and closets. He liked looking at pictures and at jewelry. He liked especially going through the clothes, sometimes commenting aloud, other times keeping his thoughts to himself.

"Wow, this is just…amazing." Charles exclaimed, pulling out a sombrero from underneath the bed. He examined it from each angle, and then started cracking up. "A sombrero? Who purposely keeps a sombrero under the fucking bed?" He glanced under the bed and exclaimed again, "It's the only thing under the entire bed! Why would anybody keep a solitary sombrero under the bed?"

I laughed, nervously taking a sip of a soda, my eyes on the door, my ears perked for any nearby footsteps. All I could hear was the faint chatter of a hundred conversations going on at once, glasses clinking with ice, faraway music pulsing through the house.

"Ugh, that is really good. This sombrero is a check plus." Charles set the sombrero on his head and continued his search.

"Let's see what else we can find. Let's see, let's see, let's see..." he continued, walking into the closet.

"What exactly," I paused quickly, hearing a crash just down the hall. A bunch of voices began to murmur, all echoing apologies. Someone yelled for paper towels and a broom. "... are you looking for?"

Charles stood up straight and glanced at me. "Nothing." He said merrily, wrapping a woman's scarf around his neck, and then unwrapping it and tossing it back into the closet. "I'm not looking for anything." Charles continued, the grin slowly fading from his face. "I guess I just like looking at the things that real people have. The things they own. The things that define them."

"You like looking at the things of real people..." I repeated. "As opposed to fictional characters?"

Charles fastened a gold watch onto his wrist. "You know what I mean, dildo. Real people. Speaking of dildos, you'd be surprised how many I've found playing this game."

"Real people?" I repeated. "Like what? Like a bus driver?"

Unfastening the watch and moving towards the opposite night stand, Charles laughed. "Sure. Why not?"

I took another sip of soda, listening to somebody yell about somebody else vomiting all over the piano in the hallway. I smiled. This guy was interested in the belongings of real people. Real people who fought all the time, who had money problems. Real people who couldn't afford braces for their kids, or got their phones cut off because they skipped a payment. Real people who had babies out of wedlock, who were on welfare. Real people, who struggled, survived, amazed, lived. Real people who were fantasizing about living the life of someone like Charles Gardensen. Real people who would kill for his belongings, his car, his house, his money, and his opportunities and this guy wanted to meet "real people."

"Why do you do this?" I asked.

He shrugged, examining a pearl necklace inside of a jewelry box. "It's nice to imagine a world, sometimes. Imagine people, their lives, their families." He paused, clearing his throat. "It's nice to believe that there's an entire world of life out there that I haven't seen or experienced yet. You know? It keeps me interested, I guess. Plus, I'm just a downright nosy bitch."

With a half-smile, I nodded, satisfied with his answer. I still didn't think it permitted him to go through peoples private belongings, but I wasn't going to be the one to take the pacifier out of the baby's mouth either.

"People are so very fascinating, Brian. Have you realized?"

I snorted. "Bums are fascinating. You should watch some of the ones that live in the alleys by my mother's apartment."

We laughed together, and then I immediately shushed myself, realizing someone could have heard us and busted Charles going through their things.

"So…what would someone find, if they were playing this game in your billionaire parents bedroom?" I asked, taking another sip of soda.

Charles stopped mid-dig, glancing over his shoulder. He bit his lip and glanced heavenward. "You would probably find…pictures of Elijah. Trinkets that belonged to him. Mementos from times when my mother and Astin were happy together. Crap that has to do or go into Astin's will. And probably newspaper clippings from when the business had first really taken off…" his voice trailed off and then he shrugged. "Yeah…" he resumed sifting through the nightstand drawer, pulling out a pair of 3D sunglasses. He smiled at them, gingerly fingering the blue and red frames. "Things were very much different between my mother and Astin when I was born. I guess you could say everything had already been said and done. The spark had lost its luster. "

I didn't know what to say. I had no idea what it was like to have a sibling. Or to live in a home with people who weren't in love anymore. I had no idea what it was to compete for affection or love. Save for luxury and money, love was one thing I never had to look for. So I didn't say anything. I continued keeping watch and sipping soda, and after a few more minutes of searching, faraway music, faint chatter, and clinking glasses, Charles pocketed the 3D sunglasses and we left.

He wore them the entire drive home.

CHAPTER 8
Charles

I wonder, a thousand times over now, how it could have happened differently.

*   *   *

It didn't feel real. Not one bit. Maybe that's why it was easy for me to do it. That and the complete disbelief of seeing the ripped out pages from my journal, the most important pages of all, falling out of her coat. Like I said. Unreal.

Most of them went for the good stuff. Expensive clothing. My watches, rings, or other jewelry. Shit, ninety percent of the time it was just straight money, right out of my wallet. A few real slick ones even managed to swipe credit cards and make purchases online. Honestly, I was used to shit like that.

But she was different. To her disadvantage. That goddamned bitch was smarter. Much smarter than all the others.

And right now all the money in the world won't fix what's wrong.

*   *   *

He's the only one who can help me. Aside from Elijah, he's the most decent person I know. And I know fucking everybody.

I knew it the other night. I was testing him. We were walking back to our dorm after a late night of barhopping with a few people we met at a concert happening downtown. I purposefully began walking ahead of him, taking quicker paces. I knew he was right behind me, walking with his eyes glued to the ground, like he usually does after a few drinks. I had been planning this for a week now.

I let the wad of hundreds fall out of my coat pocket and kept walking like I hadn't noticed at all. Our footsteps crunched in the leaves as we continued walking towards our dorm hall, but his footsteps stopped. A moment later I heard him pick up the money. He didn't say anything. He must've been counting it, shocked. There was a silence. And then nothing. I shook my head as we walked; feeling stupid for even thinking that there was a chance Brian would have done the right thing. What did I expect? He had grown up in relative filth and poverty. A thousand bucks? Maybe I should have started with five hundred.

We had made it all the way upstairs and to our room. I took my key out and just when I had given up all hope on him, he tapped my shoulder.

"You dropped this."

I turned around, astonished. "What?"

Brian nodded, tiredly. "Outside. In the leaves. I was wondering if I steal it or not, because you're such a jerk and all, but you know me…"and there it was. The money. Every single hundred dollar bill just as I had left it.

I started laughing. Brian joined in, snickering along with me. He thought I was laughing at his joke, but really, I couldn't believe it. I was shocked. Someone who wasn't looking to rip me off the first chance they could get. When you had as much money as my family did – did loyalty like that even exist anymore? I guess it didn't really matter.

Unbeknownst to him, Brian had passed one of the most important tests he would ever take during his four years at Princeton.

CHAPTER 9

Brian

"Brian, wake up," he hissed, clamping both hands on my shoulders, scaring the living hell out of me. "Wake up, *come on*."

I rolled over, trying to ignore Charles. As his roommate, I had grown accustomed to being woken up in the middle of the night over sudden urges to hit up the grocery store for ice cream, being begged to attend a last minute party, drive sixty miles away for one event or another, or make a run for a mandatory coffee and cigarettes session. It could have been anything. And any time. I pushed what I knew where Charles' hands off my shoulders and groaned. "I don't want to go out, I'm tired-"

"Listen to me," he cut me off. "Get dressed. Right now."

Now I was really pissed. I had only slept four hours the other night. I had just spent six hours doing homework and cramming for a midterm. "Charles, I don't want to go to a party right now! I'm-"

"Listen, I'm not talking about a party. Please just get

dressed. Just trust me, this is an emergency." He paused, swallowing hard. "I need you right now."

"What time is it?" I asked, sorely, rubbing my eyes. "Christ."

That was when Charles grabbed both of my arms and forced me to look into his eyes. There was a wildness in them I hadn't ever seen before. No smiles. No laughter. No jokes.

That's when I realized this was no late night coffee run.

*   *   *

"Charles, what's going on?"

"Just get in the car."

"If this is a joke, I'm going to kick your ass."

He didn't reply.

"I mean it. I won't fucking talk to you for a week, man." Nothing.

"Charles, you're freaking me out."

"Will you please just shut up, and get in the car." This wasn't a question.

"Why? What the hell is going on?"

"Just please get in." We had just reached the Porsche. Charles walked over and opened the passenger door. He held it open for me. Something he had never done before. I walked over, but didn't get in.

"Why?"

"You're the only one who can help me right now. So please, get in." We were standing in front of the passenger door of the Porsche.

"Help you, you keep saying help you, help you with that? What happened?"

Charles grabbed my collar and pulled me close to him. For a second, I thought he was going to hit me.

Pulled up close to him like that I noticed his face was flushed pink. And not only that- he was sweating.

"Listen, Brian. I will explain everything…when the time is right. Right now is not that time. Right now, I need you to listen to me. Okay? Because we're wasting valuable fucking time right now. I need you to shut up and get in the car. Can you do that, please?"

I started to tense up. He was acting so strange. During our entire friendship so far, the most serious discussion Charles and I had ever had was about which Spice Girl had ended up the most successful over the years. I stared at him, waiting for the tiniest hint of a smile to reveal that this entire get-up was a cruel practical joke. But that hint never showed.

"Please," He repeated softly, letting go of my collar, already knowing that I would say yes. We had gone this far anyway, hadn't we? I was already damned awake and dressed and standing out in the parking lot.

"Okay," I replied warily, wondering what in the hell I was signing myself up for. "Okay."

He nodded solemnly. Without saying another word, I got in the car. He quickly made his way into the passenger seat. And then we were driving into the night.

*　　*　　*

At first I had no idea where we were, but my memory struck me when I saw the faded green street sign. *Sherman Road*. This was where Charles had tried to teach me to drive his car, and told me the story of *The Lady or The Tiger*.

"What are we doing here?" I asked as the car came to a stop. Charles unbuckled his seatbelt and ignored me. He got out of the car. I followed him. We began walking down into the woods. It was really dark, naturally, since it was nearly two in the morning.

I followed Charles for a few minutes, deep into the woods. It sucked, because I couldn't see all the damn little rocks and bushes at my feet; I was too busy trying to protect my face from the myriad of tree branches. I knew better than to ask Charles what we were doing again; he hadn't spoken a word since I had gotten into the car.

A minute later he stopped, and turned around to face me.

I stopped and stared back at him. "What?"

He took a deep breath. It looked like he wanted to say something, but the only word that came out of his mouth was "Brian."

"What is it?" I asked again, trying not to sound as nervous as I really was. I was getting downright scared at this point. It was freezing and dark, and Charles was scaring the shit out of me. This was when I realized truly how little I really knew Charles Gardensen.

"Brian," he said again, clearing his throat sharply. "Whatever you do, don't scream, okay?"

Panic shot through my heart. There was such eeriness to his words that suddenly I knew he wasn't kidding me. No, this was not a joke. No matter how much I wanted it to be, this was something bad.

His eyes were shining as he stepped aside, revealing the reason we were standing in the middle of the woods at two in the morning on a cold Wednesday night.

Oh, God.

Chapter 10

Brian

At his feet was the body of a beautiful girl.

Pale.

Motionless.

Beautiful.

Dead.

I felt my breath catch in my throat.

What am I looking at?

No, no, no way…there's no way…

Before I could say anything, Charles spoke up. "Look, I can explain…but I can't do it right now. Right now I need you to help me." That was when I noticed the shovels placed on the ground behind him.

I almost laughed out loud, from sheer deniability. *The woods. Shovels? A dead beauty queen at our feet? A millionaire semi-celebrity?* "Charles," I spoke, my voice growing steadily louder, "What, what…what did you do?" Before I knew it, I was backing away from everything, from the girl lying on the cold ground, from the darkness in the woods, and from Charles' outstretched arms.

He grabbed me before I even knew I was trying to get away. "Brian," he whispered, grabbing my face with both hands. "Shhh, Brian, calm down…"

"Calm down," I cried out, trying to pry his hands off my face, unable to take my eyes off the girl lying on the ground. "Calm down! Charles, what the fuck am I looking at? Is she dead?! Is she-"

"Brian," he hissed, clamping a hand over my mouth. "Shut the fuck up, for God's sakes. You need to help me, okay? You're the only person I trust right now. You've gotta help me."

"Help you?! Help you do what?!?" I screamed, despite his warnings. He grabbed my shirt

and pulled me close to him again.

"I need you to help me get rid of her."

"Get rid of her?! Who the fuck is she?!?" I asked. Charles shoved me against a tree and

slapped my face lightly.

"Stop fucking shouting! You'll wake this entire town up. Look, there are two shovels behind me. I need you to-"

With every bit of strength I had, I shoved Charles off of me. "Are you fucking crazy or something? Look, whatever this is, I am not going to be a part of it. No way. You picked the- the wrong guy. I can't deal with this kind of shit. I can't…" my voice cracked as the realization of the situation began sinking slowly in. "Oh God, we need to call the police. Now." I began heading out towards the direction we came in when Charles grabbed my shoulder.

"Listen to me very carefully, Brian." He said, his eyes animated as I had ever seen. "That girl lying down there, got what was coming to her. Okay? Trust me on this. She had it coming. I will tell you more about what happened, but the sun will be up in three and a half hours. I need you to help me dig a fucking hole, and dump her goddamn body in it, and then bury her. I cannot do that alone. You have to help me. Okay?"

I shook my head. "No. No."

"Yes," he countered stepping closer to me.

"No. No! No fucking way! I have nothing to do with this. Nothing at all. Charles…I've never even cut a fucking class before in my life, what makes you think I can help you bury some dead girl I've never seen or met before in the fucking woods in the middle of the night?" I glanced past his shoulder to take another glance at the beautiful immobile girl lying on the ground. Eyes wide open. *Oh God*. It was real.

"I know you'll help me."

I wanted to laugh out of sheer spite. "You know I'll help you? What fucking drugs are you on, is what I'd like to know. I'm leaving. I'm calling the police. This is fucking crazy, I'm sorry, I can't help you." I turned and started walking in the direction from which we had come.

"I know you'll help me because if you don't, it's my word against yours."

I stopped in my tracks and turned around to face him. "What did you say?"

His handsome face had never been so calm, it was frightening. "How will you get back to campus? You're going to walk?" He pulled his car keys out of his pocket and jangled them in front of me. "Or are you going to knock on the first door you come across in the next five miles? You should hit a house in a little less than 2 hours. And when you do get to a phone, you're going to call the cops and tell them that Charles Gardensen, the Charles Gardensen, pulled you out of bed at 2AM to drag out to the woods and told you to help him bury a dead girl? You see, I don't think that story is going to sit well with them."

"Look Charles," I said in a surprisingly steady voice, "I'm not trying to get you in trouble or anything. But I have a future to protect. I don't even know who she was. I cannot do this. I truly cannot do this. We need to call the police and report this."

"I understand how you feel, Brian. I really do." He put his hands in his pockets. "But I don't think the police are going to really buy your story, since I used this to get into our dorm hall tonight." He pulled something out of his pocket and threw it over to me. I held out my hands and caught it. Bringing it up close to my face, I squinted to see. It was my student I.D. dorm key.

"How- how did-" A sinking feeling began to settle in my stomach. Whatever was happening, Charles had the advantage of thinking this particular scenario through. *How had he gotten a hold of my I.D key? When did I have it last? What the fuck was going on? Why was this happening to me?*

"So for all they know, it was you, dragging me out of bed, and forcing me to drive out here to help you bury a dead girl…"

I didn't say anything. He was bluffing and I knew it. There was no way they could believe that I had anything to do with this situation. I was in class all morning, and I had stayed inside my dorm and was studying all night. If I explained what happened completely and truthfully, there was no way…

"I haven't said one word about how this girl died and what

unfortunate circumstances she died under. For all you know I have nothing to do with her death. I could have merely found her like this. That fact will be very useful to the family lawyer, J.S. Vanderbilt. I'm sure you've heard of him, Brian. He's a legend. A magician in the courtroom. I should know. And you of all people know that I'll have absolutely no problems getting a few money-grubbing friends to help provide me with an alibi."

With the sinking feeling in my stomach getting worse, I realized I was fighting a losing battle.

Charles stepped closer to me. "Listen to me, Brian. I like you. I really, really, like you. You're a good person." He sighed. "Hell, I used to think my brother was as angelic as it got on Earth, but you surprise me." He ducked to avoid a branch, and came even closer to me. "In fact, you remind me of him so much...it's scary." At this point we were face to face. I was so overwhelmed with the situation, I was nearly in tears. I said nothing as he continued.

"I can help you," he whispered, staring into my eyes. "I can give you anything you want. My word is as good as gold. And you know it. Let's face it – this country loves my family." He paused for a second, emitting a bitter laugh. "As fucked up as that sounds, we both know it's true. And between Joe Blow from Stratton Street and a Gardensen, you don't stand a chance against me." He paused to take a breath, which formed as a visible little cloud from the cold. "But if you're with me...I can make anything you want happen. With a few words, with the blink of an eye, with the nod of my head, I can make you somebody, Brian. I can make you somebody before you know it." His eyes gleamed with intensity as I listened to his words, halfheartedly. I glanced at the lifeless girl a few feet away and felt like crying. A losing battle. "I can make anything you want happen. What about your poor mother back home whose working two jobs and sixty hours a week? How about we send her a little money, huh? How about you? We both know you could use a little financial boost. We both know you're too good to steal it from me, huh?" He gave a bitter laugh. "You've had plenty of chances to do that, yet you never have." I closed my eyes, realizing all those times he had left money laying around, or conveniently dropped money for me to pick up... he was testing me.

"Charles," I pleaded as a final attempt, "please don't make me do this. Please. I won't even tell the police. I swear. I just want to go home. I just want to get on with everything. I don't want to do this. Charles, I don't even know who she was. I-"

"Look, all I can tell you right now is that she was a bad person. She was a bad person with no morals and she ran with a terrible crowd and she's exactly where she should be. When you understand the truth, you'll be glad you helped me, Brian." He nodded, earnestly.

I shook my head, feeling sick to my stomach. "I can't help you do this, Charles. I can't. This...I can't be a part of this. Let me go and I won't ever mention it again, I swe"

"And if I really have to hurt you, Brian, I can," he whispered softly against my face, cutting me off. "You know what good friends Astin is with the higher ups at Princeton, don't you? You know that I report anything stolen, or missing, and they happen to find it on you, which they might, you'll get kicked out of school and lose your scholarship, don't you? You know if they find the drugs hidden in your room, there goes your scholarship. So think about this really carefully before you walk away from me. Like I said, it'll be my word against yours."

A strange lethargy overcame my entire body. Everything I had worked for my entire life flashed before my eyes. All those nights studying. All those lonely afternoons, at the library. My salutatorian speech. My mother crying with pride. Staring at everybody who had money for the snack bar after school. The hunger in my stomach. The rocks underneath my thin soles. And I stared at him. Everything I wasn't. Inside and out. "Why me?" I asked, softly, already knowing that he had won.

"You were the only one I could trust." Charles replied, simply. "Put these on." He said, handing me a pair of gloves. He walked over to the shovels and pulled out a pair of shoes. Size 13. "And put these on over your shoes. And hurry up. We only have three hours now."

CHAPTER 11
Charles

We finished burying the body about 40 minutes before sunrise. I knew I couldn't have done it alone…Shit. Everything got fucked up. Fucked the hell up. Brian didn't say anything the entire time. He just kept digging alongside me, wiping his eyes and nose every now and then; I think he was in shock still. Whatever. I didn't expect it to be a fucking wonderful social escapade anyway.

We walked back to the car in complete silence. I had lined the inside of my trunk with plastic bags. Wordlessly I placed the shovels in the trunk.

"Give me your gloves." I said to Brian. He was staring off into the horizon, as if waiting for the sun to show itself and expose us right then and there. "Brian. The gloves." I repeated, impatiently. He peeled them off and handed them over.

"Take off your shoes."

Without saying a word, he slipped out of the size thirteen sneakers I had handed him.

"Take off your clothes."

Brian looked up at me.

"I'm serious. I need your clothes. All of them. Everything. Take it off." I reached into the trunk and handed him a pair of jeans and a sweater. "Take those clothes off and put these on."

"Whose clothes are those?" he asked, tiredly.

"They're mine. Now just put them on." I said, getting anxious. I wanted to be out of there already. I turned around to give Brian his privacy as he changed clothing. When he was done, he handed the clothes over and I tossed them into the trunk along with the shoes. *What else? What else? What else was I forgetting?*

"Get in the car. We're going." I said, unlocking both doors. Silently, Brian let himself in the car. The seatbelt noise began going off and I didn't give two shits. In fact, it would be wonderful if a semi came crashing into us and that was the end of it. I would be so lucky, huh? I left the seatbelt unfastened and we drove, *beep beep, beep beep, beep beep,* every two minutes.

"When we get to the dorm, I'll give you your I.D card back, okay?" I said, trying to lighten the tension in the car up. It was so thick it made dinner with my mother and Astin seem as delightful and carefree as getting ice cream on a summer afternoon.

Staring out the window at the passing trees, Brian ignored me.

"When we get back, I need you to take a shower, okay?"

Again, silence.

"Do you want to say anything?"

Nothing.

"You hate me?"

Nothing.

"You shouldn't."

Nothing.

"You should tell yourself you had no choice."

Nothing.

"You should tell yourself that you made the best possible decision for that situation."

Nothing.

"Just when we get home, take a shower, and relax. I'll take care of everything else."

Nothing.

I swallowed hard. The bastard wasn't making it any easier for me. I didn't want to drag him into this. Driving back, I gripped the steering wheel so hard my knuckles were turning white. *What had I done? What had I just fucking done?*

"Who was she?"

"Huh?" I asked, brought back to life by the sound of Brian's voice.

"That girl," he said, his voice cracking. "Who was she?"

I bit my lip, wondering exactly what to tell him, and exactly what to omit, or lie about. I had thought about only for a minute before this whole mess had happened, and so it wasn't sorted out in my head. Regardless, I had to say something. "She was someone I met after my brother died. She…was… sort of an old girlfriend."

"Jesus Christ," Brian muttered under his breath.

"No, it wasn't like that," I said, noticing a speed limit sign for 45. I slowed down to match it. Fuck if I got pulled over with all that shit in my trunk. Not that I had met any officer who cared to offend Astin like that. "We weren't close. She wasn't a good person, Brian. She used me."

Brian didn't say anything.

I continued, feeling the need to keep explaining. "She pretended to like me, and pretended to give a shit about how torn up I was over Elijah's...death." I felt myself getting angry all over again. "But...she turned on me. She fucked me over real bad. I found out she was stealing from me."

Brian scoffed. "She stole from you, so you fucking killed her? I thought everybody stole from you. How many other people have you buried?"

I shook my head. "Nobody. Nobody else. Just her."

"What made her so special?"

I swallowed again, deciding that there was no real way around it. Brian was no retard, and I was hesitant to try and lie to him. *Fuck it.* "She knew a secret about me."

For a minute, he didn't say anything. He was probably trying to figure out if I was bullshitting him or not. I kept my eyes on the road, and coughed before continued. "She was stealing from me, and one day, while she was going through my stuff, she found something out about me, about my family. She asked me to meet her one day. I did. She revealed that she knew this secret about my family, and unless I gave her ten grand, she was going to call up the local papers and tell them all about it."

Brian remained silent, but I could tell he was still listening.

"So guess what? I fucking got the money and gave it her. Just like she asked. And she swore that she would never mention anything about this secret again. I gave her the money and she gave me back the proof she found about our secret. I told her to lose my number, to leave me alone, and we were done and finished forever. I told her I couldn't believe she'd take advantage of me and threaten my family with more drama and press after the loss of Elijah. She said it was a tough world out there, and not everyone was as blessed as I was. She gave me some bullshit quote by some Italian guy, about doing what you have to do in life…in order to get what you want."

"Machiavelli. The ends justify the means."

I glanced over at him, unsure at why I was surprised. "Yeah. That one."

Brian continued staring out the window. "Then what happened?"

I bit my lip angrily. "What do you think happened, Brian? You think we all went on our merry little ways and that's why she's buried in those fucking woods out there? The ten grand lasted her about 6 months." I paused, clearing my throat. "Then she came back."

"She came back, of course, but this time, she wanted twenty grand, or else she was going to go to the press with our secret. I thought I had gotten back all the proof she had, but it turns out the little bitch had made copies. And so I was back at square one. And so I paid her again. But she came back. And this little routine has been plaguing me for three years now, and the payoff for her silence was getting way too steep. And what if I paid her the money again, it was no guarantee that she wouldn't just open her fucking mouth one day and let everybody know what she knows anyway? And what it somebody found the proof she had supposedly had so many copies of? Then what? I couldn't risk having a loose end like that. So it's taken me a while to realize that this was the only way to get rid of this problem. Isn't that right? You do what you have to do? Huh, Brian?"

He remained silent. "She's the one who's been calling you, texting you lately?"

I nodded silently. A moment passed. "How come you haven't asked me yet?"

Brian turned his head to look at me. "Asked you what?"

I didn't say anything.

"Asked you what?"

"You know, if I were you and sitting in your seat over there, and you were me, and I had just helped you bury some blackmailing sonofabitch over some big terrible secret, I would want to know what that secret was, you know?"

Brian shook his head. "You will never know what it is like to be me and be sitting where I'm sitting."

"You aren't even the smallest bit curious?"

Brian shook his head.

"In some sick weird way, I want to tell you, you know..." I admitted. "I want to tell you so you'd better understand why I did what I had to do, and why I needed you to help me. But we both know I can't do that, huh?" I asked, giving a sardonic chuckle.

"You're damn right you can't. I don't want to know any part of it. Look, just let me out here. I'll walk the rest of the way." We had just pulled up to the campus.

"Were you listening to anything I said back there? I need to make sure you get upstairs and take a shower, first things first." I lucked out and found a parking spot relatively quickly. "So stick with the plan."

Wordlessly, we both got out of the car. I locked the doors and followed Brian, who was walking much quicker ahead than I was. When we got to the dorm hall, I handed him his student I.D, which he swiped to give us entry. I followed him up the stairs and waited patiently as he fumbled with the lock. A moment later we were inside.

"Look, you just take a shower and relax for a while, okay? I've got one more thing to take care of and then I'll be back so we can discuss arrangements for you. Okay?" I put my arms on his shoulders. "You really saved my ass back there, Brian. I mean it. And in a little while you're going to thank yourself for it. There are big rewards in store for you. Okay?"

He didn't say anything. Instead he pulled my hands off his shoulders and walked into the bathroom, shutting the door hard behind him.

CHAPTER 12

Brian

Standing in the shower, I had turned the water as hot as I could stand it and let it beat on my body. I stood there, eyes closed, repeatedly asking myself the same question.

Why didn't I go to Yale? I should have gone to Yale. Shit, Community College would have been better than this. I'm sure I would have been just as successful in life had I gone to Yale. Shit. Shit. Shit. What do I do? What can I do? What are my options? Think, think, think…

Okay, he's gone. He had to take care of one other thing. Whatever the fuck that means. He's probably getting rid of all the stuff in his trunk. His trunk. Which was lined with plastic or something. Crap. God, I can't believe just a few hours ago I was sitting here studying for a test and doing homework. How stupid and trivial an exam seems like right now. Of all the roommates in the world, Jesus Christ- no, okay, let's not start with that. What I have to do right now is think. I have a little time, which is good. Great, even. Okay. So. What do I need right now? Besides a fucking time machine and a really strong mixed drink? Help. I need help. I need to tell someone too. I have to report him. I need to get away from him and report him. Okay. So how do I do that?

He said he was going to come back in a little it so we could discuss 'arrangements'. Fuck, I don't want any arrangements! I just want to this nightmare to be over. I want to wake up. Arrangements will just make this entire thing more disgusting, more real, more inescapable. I can't take anything from him. That will make it more real, and make me more of an accomplice, when what really happened is I was fucking sitting here minding my business when he came in and dragged me in the middle of nowhere and basically forced me to help him bury some dead girl. Would that story work? It's not even a story- it's the fucking truth! Do I have any proof? What could I pin against him? He made me wear gloves and huge shoes, shoes that don't match either of our foot sizes. He made me wear different clothes. He has all of the stuff with him. He brought the shovels too. I wonder if he was stupid enough to charge the shovels to a credit card of some sort…No. Probably not. He had the hindsight to use different clothes, shoes, and protect fingerprints with gloves, there is no way he would overlook charging shovels to a credit card. Or would he?!?What about the girl's family? Won't they report her missing? Then what? Do they know she was blackmailing him? Will they know to have the police question Charles about it? Would the police even do it? Jesus, what secret is worth murdering someone over? No- let's not even open that can of worms. Okay, think, Brian, think…

Should I call the police first? Or Campus Security? Or my mom? Would my mom know what to do? No. God. She'd probably think I was on drugs. She'd tell me to take a hot bath and lay down. She is another fan of the Gardensen family. Great. Okay, definitely not my mom. Mom, out. Police? No. No, I'll go to

Campus Security first. I'll go there, since this sort of started and ended on campus…right? I'll go there and I'll tell them the entire truth. God, that wouldn't make me an accomplice, would it?! I was acting under duress! He forced me into it. He threatened me with everything I worked so hard for. He threatened to get me kicked out of school and have my scholarship revoked. He threatened me with his social status. He dragged me to the middle of the woods; it would have been miles before I could have gotten back to campus, in which situation he could have easily out-driven me. Is J.S Vanderbilt really as good as an attorney as they say he is? Does Charles really know people who would vouch for his alibi for a little bit of money? Yes, and Yes. Oh God. Could he really twist this whole thing back on me? Would they really do that to me? Well, there's a dead girl buried back in the woods not too far from here over some blackmailing secret, so I'm going to go out on a limb with YES. There's no saying with people like Charles and what they do to people like you and me if we get in their way…God, can you believe he was LAUGHING back there? He cracked a joke and then laughed about it? How could any sane person laugh at a time like this? Maybe…maybe that was a defense mechanism. Yeah, maybe he was just trying to seem like he was okay with what had just happened when he was really like, shitting bricks, just to make sure I wouldn't notice, because if I knew he was as scared as I was, I probably would have opened the door and jumped out of the car while he was doing 70 on the freeway. Yeah. No, wait, why am I defending him? It's ME I should be worried about it. My ass is on the line here. My future, my life, God, I haven't even ever had sex yet. I can't go out like this. I can't go to prison, and I don't want this to be it. There's still so much to be experienced. This is it. It's over. If I don't do something now, I'll regret it for the rest of my life. At the very least I need to transfer schools, and if I do then I'll lose an entire semester so fuck it, right? Right. Okay. As soon as I get out of this shower, I'm going to Campus Police. I am going to tell them the truth. Everything. Okay. Here goes.

I turned off the water, my skin bright red from the heat, and stepped out of the shower. I wrapped a towel around myself and unlocked the bathroom door. I was going to get dressed and get it over with. My mind was made up. I got dressed quickly and started heading out the door when I saw the door to Charles' bedroom was slightly open. I stared at it for a moment. Another moment. And another. And then I found myself walking over to his bedroom door, pushing it all the way open, and stepping inside.

What, oh, what could I find in here that would make my story more believable? I wondered, as I stepped through half-eaten apples, opened and unopened packs of cigarettes, the different scents of many colognes mingling, and an array of designer clothes tossed everywhere. The bed was unmade and there were names and phone numbers scrawled all over little pieces of paper and even the wall.

I walked over to his closet and opened it. Just clothes. And hats. And shoes. Size 11. Not thirteen like he had cleverly used. Belts. Ties. More boxes of colognes. I opened the boxes of colognes, went through the shirts and shoe boxes… Nothing. Nada.

I walked over to the bed and got on my hands and knees. As much of a slob as Charles was, he managed to keep underneath his bed spotless. There was nothing there.

"Freak." I said, out loud.

I walked over to his dresser. Maybe he had something to connect him to the girl!? It was a worth a shot. An old photograph? A phone number? Crap. A phone number wouldn't help because I didn't even know her name, and honestly, I was started to forget her face. Selective memory, I guess. Regardless, I rifled through the first drawer. Nothing. The second drawer, nothing. The third drawer was clothing, and so was the fourth. I rifled through the clothes in the fifth drawer and all of a sudden my fingers hit something smooth and solid. *What?* I felt out underneath the piles of pants and jeans and felt it again. Something definitely in there. I grabbed whatever it was with both hands and pulled it out from underneath the countless pairs of pants.

Oh, yes….oh yes, oh yes, oh yes.

A few minutes later I grabbed the phone and punched in Charles cell phone number. He picked up on the first ring.

"Meet me at Carson's Restaurant at 10 O'clock tonight." It was all I said before I hung up.

CHAPTER 13
Brian

I was nervous as I had ever been in my life. Half of me didn't even expect him to show, and the other half sort of didn't want him to. I was never good a social situations, much less social confrontation. I sat there in the booth, looking at my digital wristwatch, and tapping my foot. Nervous. Nervous. Nervous. *Maybe he won't show. Maybe he didn't even hear what I said on the phone and I'll be sitting here all night for no reason.* It was 10:10 P.M. *Maybe he –*

"Is this the part where you tell me you've been tape recording all of our conversations since Day 1?" I turned around and there he was. Charles Gardensen. Standing there, looking slightly tired, and still making attempts at humor on a night like this.

I waited for him to sit down, but he continued standing there, a strange half-smile on his face. He was starting to freak me out. Why was he still standing? After almost a minute, I spoke.

"Sit down, Charles." I said, trying very hard to keep my voice from quavering.

With a sigh, Charles lowered his body into the booth. He rubbed his eyes and the waiter came by.

"What'll it be tonight, guys?"

I shook my head. "I'm fine."

"Double vodka tonic on the rocks."

The waiter nodded. "Certainly. I'll be right back and give you guys another moment to look at the menu."

Charles shook his head. "That won't be necessary; the drink will be enough, thank you."

The waiter nodded again. "Of course, I'll be back in a moment."

Charles scratched the back of his neck. "Don't do anything stupid, Brian. Please."

"Stupid?" I asked, hating the fact that my voice was an octave higher than usual. "Stupid like what?"

"Stupid like pass up on a once-in-a-lifetime opportunity that I'm about to give you."

"I don't want anything from you Charles. You shouldn't have involved me in this. It's too bad you did." I said, trying to sound as solid as my words. He stared at me, eyes narrowed. I couldn't tell if he was buying it or not.

"Brian, Brian, Brian. You're not so sure you want to do this, are you?"

"I'm sure."

Charles reached inside his coat and pulled something out of it. A checkbook.

"How's a hundred grand sound?"

Oh God, *one hundred thousand dollars.* I shook my head. *No, no, no.* "I - I brought you here for a reason, Charles."

"I already know what reason."

"Oh yeah?" I asked, reaching into my coat and pulling out diary I had found in his bottom drawer, the same diary I had stumbled across when Charles had first moved into the dorm.

Charles flinched at the sight of it.

"You know, from what I've seen in here, there's enough to connect you with her. You noted some days and figures in here, which could easily could be the pay offs. Which supports your story of being blackmailed. Which gives you a motive to have gotten rid of her, Charles." I said, holding very tightly onto his diary, still not really feeling the reality of my words or the moment.

"So you read my diary then?"

"Not all of it. Just enough."

Charles chuckled. "Well, maybe you should have read all of it. Then maybe you'd notice how fucked up my thoughts are. You know, it was the doctor's idea to start keeping a diary. That was around the same time he started prescribing me a shitload of pills. Right after my brother died."

I remained silent.

"Also, you probably know that my diary would be inadmissible evidence in a court of law, because you stole it from me, when it was clearly in my property."

I swallowed hard. "It doesn't matter. It's still proof."

"Those dates and figures could be anything."

"They're payoffs. Dates and amounts. You were keeping track."

"You don't understand, Brian."

"I don't even want to."

"You wouldn't be so quick to rat me out if you knew the whole truth."

"I don't want the truth. I just want my conscience back. I can't live with what you've made me do."

"How much, Brian?"

Confused, I willed myself to stare at him."How much what?"

"Everybody has their price. And you're no different, are you, Brian Walden from Stratton street? Brian Walden whose mother is a hairdresser and works almost 60 hours a week to keep a roof over your head? Brian Walden who jumped at the chance to walk in my shoes, to be my friend, to share my luxuries. So just cut this fucking Boy Scout act out and tell me what I need to do to make this work out for both of us."

Just then the waiter returned with Charles' drink. "Anything else, gentlemen?"

"One more of these." Charles said, finishing the drink in one long sip. He tapped his empty glass on the table. The waiter smiled and walked away. He was probably thinking about the huge tip Charles was going to leave him. Funnily enough, that night was the only night in his life where Charles Gardensen didn't leave a tip.

We sat there silently until the waiter brought over Charles' second drink. Charles lit a cigarette and then took a long sip of his drink. He set the glass down on the table. Folding his hands, he looked at me. "What do you want to happen, Brian?"

I paused, realizing that I wasn't completely sure. I didn't want any money. But I did want money. I didn't want to be linked to this nightmare, but that was too late. I had truly liked Charles up until last night, and I didn't necessarily want him to serve a life sentence in prison for what he had done. Yet I didn't want him to roam the streets and campus freely. I didn't want to be his roommate anymore for damn sure. I didn't want to make problems. I just wanted to get out of this. Before I could say anything, Charles slid over a small slip of paper across the table.

I glanced down at it. It was one of the friendship coupons from the booklet I had given him a few weeks ago. *Good for One Truth Session!* I just stared at it. I wanted to laugh. I wanted to cry. Before I could react to it, he slid another small piece of a paper across the table. This one was a picture. A young adult male. Dark hair. Dark eyes. Square jaw. There was a kindness to his eyes. A slight smile on his lips.

"Do you ever wonder why we don't look alike?" Charles asked, taking a drag of his cigarette. He began fiddling with the small stirrer in his empty glass. "Me and Elijah?"

I shrugged, having no idea where he was going with the question. "Is this your brother?"

Charles nodded. "We don't spend the holidays together anymore, my family. Mother keeps making these excuses about Astin having business trips, or some other emergency, but we both know the truth." he cleared his throat. "After Elijah died, nothing at home was ever the same, and Astin didn't care to spend any time with the rest of us. I wonder how many more years my mother is going repeat those lies to various guests at different parties. I imagine there was a point in time where they were very in love with each other, and they were happy together. I think I've seen about ten pictures of them together, where they look really happy together. Half of those pictures are taken with Elijah, him just being born. After I was born, there's this… distance …between them in the photographs.

You wouldn't have to know them to notice it. And as I grew up, so did that distance between them."

I sat very still, an eerie feeling creeping over my body. "I'm sorry, Charles."

"I know your mind is made up, Brian. I know you don't want to cover up what we did. But before you decide to do anything, I'm going to tell the truth. I'm going to make you understand. It's all I got left. If you still want to turn me in after you hear this, then fine. But I've got to try."

Keeping my eyes on the photograph of Charles' brother, I didn't say anything.

"My brother…was the American dream come true." He said, snorting through his words. "You know. I mean, you know, he was…he was…everything I am not." A look came over Charles face, a sort of glazed-over look; as if he wasn't really all with me. "And you can imagine we had the typical bullshit labels everyone expected us to have, he was the wiser, older, good son, and I was the brat, the annoying, the troublemaking bad son. No matter what though, he always stuck up for me." Charles laughed slowly. "I never fucking understood that about him. I would do something stupid, like make a huge mess or break something valuable, sometimes accidentally, most of the time on purpose, and my mother would get upset and Astin would be screaming…and Elijah would protect me. He would take the blame. Say something like, he wasn't watching me, so it was his fault, or even sometimes lie and say he had done it, when it was always me. He would save me. He would do it a lot, when we were young. When we got older, I would do other stupid things…and he would try to help me still. Hide my mistakes for me. Do my homework. Hide the drugs, the liquor. Whatever it was, he would try to help." Charles paused, lifting the empty shot glass to his lips. He looked up at me, his eyes watery. "You know, all those years I kept trying to figure out why he was always helping me, why he always stood up for me, why he looked out for me so much."

He didn't say anything for a moment; he began playing with the cap of his lighter. He flicked it open and closed. Open and closed, open and closed. "She found out, is what happened. She found out and she wasn't supposed to." I could hear the tone of his voice sliding dangerously. He began flicking the lighter open and closed faster and faster.

"What did she find out, Charles?" I asked, gently. I wanted to put my arm on his shoulder, but I was afraid to touch him.

He looked up at me, his eyes wet with emotion. "Don't you get it, genius?! Don't you understand yet? For someone whose supposed to be as smart as you are, Jesus Christ…"

"What, what is it? What haven't I figured out?" I asked, aggravated.

"How much more Astin loved Elijah than me, how my mother is a total fucking zombie who dopes herself up every day, how they've tried to keep me out of the family affairs and the family business my entire life, how Elijah and I don't even look alike!? Don't you get it?" He leaned forward, his hand balling in and out of a fist. And then he lowered his voice to a menacing whisper. "Astin Gardensen isn't my father."

I sat back, stunned.

Charles rubbed his temples gingerly, before continuing. "Elijah is my half-brother. My mother had an affair after Elijah was born. Astin was so busy overseas. He'd leave her alone for weeks at a time, spending every free minute on his newborn son, or his work. She was angry at him for putting her last, angry at being ignored and was finally realizing money wasn't an excuse for a life without love…they had been high school sweethearts…" he paused, his voice cracking slightly. "He promised her she'd always be the most important thing to him. A year went by and then another and soon he was too successful and involved in his business to keep his promise to her. She couldn't handle the loneliness after awhile and had an affair behind his back with some fucking handyman who fixed things around the mansion. And nine magical fucking months later I was born."

I wrung my hands together as I tried to say something, but he continued before I could think of anything to say. "And Astin, as much of an asshole as he is, let's face it, is no dummy,"

I looked around, realizing there were no other patrons at the restaurant. "And the more and more he thinks about it and does the math and realizes he wasn't anywhere near my mother during the month I was conceived." Charles smiled frighteningly. "So he figures it out! And he questions her about it. And she breaks down like he knew she would and admits the truth! She tells him the truth, tells him she was lonely and I was never supposed to happen." He laughed sardonically. "The doomed, Brian! God knows who we are, yes he does, but it doesn't mean he's going to save us!" He slammed his fist on the table. "And the only reason Astin doesn't get rid of my mother is because their two and a half year old son absolutely loves her. Yes, my sweet older half-brother absolutely loves mommy. So he keeps her around for Elijah. So that Elijah can have a mother and a father. And since she's four months pregnant and starting to show, they can't fucking get rid of me! It's too late! And so they decide to just raise me as their child, making it so that my entire existence is a constant reminder of her infidelity to him and his broken promise of a happy life to her!"

I sat back in shock as Charles continued. "And so I spend my childhood wondering why my dad doesn't want to play with me, why he doesn't ever want to hold me or talk to me, spend time with me, love me!" A small tear traced down his face, but he wiped it away quickly. "I was only a little boy, Brian. How was I supposed to know that every time I looked at him, smiled at him, all he saw was her the product of his wife's betrayal?"

I sat there, stunned at this admission. "Charles...I-"

He ignored me, continuing. "So I spent a large part of my life trying to gain love and approval that I would never feel or see. And Elijah...he knew. You see, he knew the entire time. And I used to think he really loved me...but thinking about it now, I'm sure it was just pity. He knew the truth and he felt sorry for me. That's why he was so nice to me. That's why he tried to save me. Because he knew the truth. And one week while Astin was out of town, I stole the keys to his Bentley to go and try and impress some girls I met at school. I was sixteen. I picked them up. We got drunk and fooled around for a few hours in someone's basement. Then we went driving around town in the Bentley. I was drunk and ended up crashing and wrecking the entire front of the car. One of the girls hit her head pretty bad. I sprained my wrist. The cops showed up. They were too scared to really arrest me, so all they did was drive me to the police station and call my house to see if someone could pick me up."

"An hour or two later, Elijah showed up. Only this time he didn't have any kind words for me, or a shoulder to cry on. On the drive home he accused me of being weak, a weak spineless bastard who didn't care about anyone except himself. I tried to tell him to shut up, leave me alone…I was crying, and he was…disgusted at me, telling me to be a man, and that people were much worse off than myself. When we got home, I tried to lock myself in my bedroom but he followed me up the stairs, still shouting at me. I told him to go fuck himself and that he could only preach to me from his wonderful side of the fence. That was when he finally stopped yelling. He told me I was right, and admitted that we were raised and treated differently our entire lives. He told me it wasn't my fault. He told me that I deserved just as much from our parents as he did. I got angry then. I began throwing things, asking him why, why were things so different then? What had I done for Astin to dislike me so much? Why both our parents could barely stand to hold me as a child, or even pay attention to me now?"

"And then he finally broke down and told me the truth. That is wasn't my fault. That our mother had an affair. That I was an accident. That Astin wasn't my father."

"I didn't believe him. I didn't want to believe him even though I knew right away he was telling me the truth. I started shoving him. He tried to calm me down. I was so angry. We were right at the edge of the stairs…I didn't mean to, I really," Charles looked up into my eyes, earnestly, "you've got to believe me when I say this, Brian, you are the only person I've ever told. I really didn't mean to-" his voice cracked and he began breaking down, "kill him, I fucking didn't mean to do it. I only wanted to hurt him. Push him. I pushed him real hard and he fell… I didn't think he was going to fall down the stairs and break his fucking neck the way he did. I-, I-," his voice broke into sobs.

I sat across from him dumbfounded, not knowing how

to react to anything, every minute leaving me more stunned than the last.

"It was an accident, it was an accident, and that's the truth. When the ambulance showed up to take him away, I told them…I told them he fell. They believed me. They sent me to a psychiatrist to help me deal with what happened, but… after that it was all over. My life lost all meaning. I tried to kill myself once at the house, afterwards, and they made me stay at some hospital for two weeks. Astin paid off so many reporters and so much hospital staff to keep quiet about my stay."

"She found out…" I said softly…"It was in your diary?"

Charles closed his eyes. "People were always stealing my fucking clothes, and money, and whatever else, I never thought anybody would steal a diary. No one cared about what I thought or how I felt for so many years. You should've seen the look on her face when I caught her. Like she struck gold. She knew, Brian…she knew, " he stared at me. "She knew how much that diary and those words and that story could be worth…The perfect family. A bastard son, an unfaithful wife, an accidental death over a terrible secret. She knew the world would eat it up with a spoon. She knew she could blackmail me for the rest of my life to keep Astin and everyone from knowing that Elijah was dead because… because of me. And when we met, I was beginning to think I could finally put it behind me. I didn't need my family, because I had found a friend. I found someone who chose to love me instead of believing they had to simply because I was related to them" His eyes met mine briefly before he continued. "I knew as long as she was alive…she would be my constant reminder of that horrible night…she would be famous for exposing the truth about the Gardensens." He stopped speaking, and pressed his fingers to his temples. "She had a grandmother on welfare. She was already talking numbers minutes after I caught her."

I breathed out heavily, not having an inkling of how to deal with anything Charles had just laid out for me. He sighed. "It's a real shame, you know, because I really liked you, Brian. I wasn't lying when I said you reminded me of Elijah. You really are more like him than you'll ever know." He sat back in his chair and rubbed his temples. "So there it is. The truth. You're the only person in the entire world who knows now. She would have ruined my life, Brian. You know it."

I bit my lip hard. I was overwhelmed with sadness for Charles, the life he lived, the emptiness that the papers and the press never showed. The sadness that was his family. The loveless gorgeous mansion they lived in. The guilt he had lived with for ending his brother's life. Despite my sorrow for Charles, I still wanted Charles to come clean about the girl he had made me help him bury.

"As sorry as I am for what you've been through, I still need to do this, Charles. We need to confess."

He nodded, another tear running down his face. He swiped at it quickly. "Are you sure?"

I nodded slowly. "I can do it with you, or without you. I hope...I hope you'll come with me." I said, not realizing that I felt that way until that very moment.

Charles didn't say anything for a moment. We sat there in silence. The waiter came by again, took away Charles' empty second glass and left.

Charles finally looked up at me. "Okay. Let's go." He stood up.

I stood up after him, and we walked out of the restaurant slowly. Charles' car was parked across the street.

"Let's walk, okay?" he said, telling me more than asking me.

"Okay," I answered, not wanting to argue that it was fifteen blocks to the Campus Police building and it was really cold outside. I felt like I owed it to him, I guess.

We walked for a minute before he spoke. "I wonder what will happen to me."

I remained silent, not sure what to say.

"I'd rather die than go to prison."

I jammed my hands into the thin pockets of my coat, wishing we would get there faster.

I never saw it coming.

"I want to thank you Brian, for being the only person," he reached his hand into his coat pocket, "who never let me buy them out." And then he hit me.

Before everything went black, I saw his overstretched hand hurtling down towards the back of my head, something dark and heavy in it.

*   *   *

I woke up a few minutes later, wondering if I had dreamt the entire crazy scene between Charles and myself. When I saw the group of people standing over me with worried expressions on their faces, I knew it had really happened.

"Are you all right?" one of the girls in the group asked, leaning over me. "We called an ambulance. You've been lying here for awhile."

I slowly sat up, realizing a very sharp pain on the side of my head. Touching it, I winced. My fingers came back with blood on them. "Oh, God," the girl standing over me said out loud. My head ached terribly. "They'll be here really soon, okay, don't worry."

"Can you stand up just yet, or does it still hurt too much?" Someone else asked me. I hesitated, pushing myself up higher with my arms. "I think I can stand."

"Here, I'm going to help you, okay? On three, we're going to stand. One, two, three." The girl slipped her hands under my armpits and pulled me up. I groaned my head killing me. She helped me limp over to the corner of the sidewalk, where I sat up against the wall.

I looked up at her through the pain. "Thanks." I said, breathing heavily.

She smiled at me. "You're welcome. What happened to you?"

Before I could answer her, we heard the sirens of an ambulance in the distance.

"Ah, that would be the paramedics coming then."

I nodded. "Right."

"My name is Mina."

"Brian."

"I hope you're all right, Brian." Mina said, as the ambulance pulled up to us. She rejoined her group of friends as two paramedics came out towards me.

"You all right?" one of them asked, squinting at the spot on my head where Charles had hit me.

I shrugged. "My head really hurts."

"What happened?"

"Somebody hit me."

"In the head?"

I nodded, breathing heavily.

"All right son, come along with me. Here, hold onto my shoulders." A minute later I was sitting in the back of the ambulance, watching Mina and her friends standing at the

very spot where Charles had clocked me in the head with…
whatever the hell he had hidden in his pocket.

I felt a sudden rush of dizziness. *Did that all really just
happen? Seriously?* Another EMT got into the back with me.
"All right, honey, lay down on the stretcher. We're going to
check you out and make sure you're okay. We're taking you
to the hospital, okay? Don't worry."I nodded weakly, feeling
overwhelmed. The EMT helped me onto the stretcher and
secured me in. A minute later we were off and before I knew
it, I had fallen out of consciousness again.

* * *

"You're awake!"I gently opened and closed my eyes,
adjusting them to the light. I glanced down at myself. I was
wearing a white gown. In a bed with white sheets. I looked to
the left. White walls. I looked to my right and saw a beaming
nurse in white scrubs. She laughed gaily. "How do you feel,
honey?"

I licked my lips. I felt a dull throbbing in the back of my
head. "Okay. My head kind of hurts."

"Oh, I bet it does, poor thing. You've got a nice big lump
on the side of your head."

"How long have I been here?"

"Just overnight. Hold on; let me see if I can get something
to make your head

feel better. I know your doctor is running around here
somewhere. Hang on, okay? " She sailed out of the room,
humming to herself.

I lay there staring at my surroundings when the events of
last night played back in my head, forwards, backwards, in
snippets, over and over. No matter how many times I went
over it, nothing felt real.

The nurse returned to the room with a little cup of ice water and two pills. "Here you go honey, this is just a little headache medicine. Go on and take those." I nodded, accepting the cup of water and the pills.

"How long do I have to stay here?"

The nurse paused, scrunching her face in thought. "The doctor would prefer at least 24 hours, they ran a cat scan and an MRI, but luckily you have no internal swelling. Just a cut and nice big lump."

I nodded weakly. "I see."

She smiled. "All right, sugar. Go ahead and relax. Just press that little button if you need anything else, all right?"

"Thank you."

I fade out.

*   *   *

The cop whistled. "Quite a temper that Gardensen kid has."

Charles. "Where is he now?" I asked.

The cop shook his head. "He ran off right after he knocked you out. Took the gun with him. We got people looking for him right now." I nodded slightly, trying not to move my head up and down too much. "I'm Officer Raymond. What's your name, son?" "Brian. Brian Walden."

"All right, Brian, I know this may be kind of hard right now, since you've been badly injured, but it's best to report as many details as you can remember about what happened as soon as possible, while the facts are still fresh in your mind. So what exactly happened between you and Mr. Gardensen that led up to the altercation between the both of you? Tell me anything and everything you remember." He sat with a pen in his hands, poised right over a notepad. I sat up in the hospital bed…realizing this was exactly what Charles was talking about. The police, the reporters, the newspapers, the TV anchors…this is all what they would go after. This is what they all wanted. A beautiful story of family and the American dream gone wrong. A miserable multi-millionaire. A beautiful adulterous wife. An innocent dead son. A mentally unstable role-model-gone-wrong. A secret. A tragedy. A murder.

"Son?" Even if Serena McCauley's grandmother found out who took her granddaughter away from her, it still wouldn't bring her back. Perhaps it was best to not put a face on the one who took her only family away. "Brian?"And Astin and Charles' mother had already been heartbroken countless times by Charles, regardless of whether he was at fault or not… did they also really need to live knowing that their son was responsible for a missing dead girl at the university? They had been through enough as a family. It would probably ruin Astin and do his mother in. Was this worth my fifteen minutes of fame? Was this worth being interviewed by all the biggest papers and talk shows and having my face in the picture? Yeah, they'd pay, they'd all pay through the roof with the kind of information Charles had left me with.

Was it worth it?

"Hey, kid?"I looked up at the officer.

"Yes, sir?"

"You spacing out on me?"

I shook my head. "Sorry, my head still hurts pretty bad."

He nodded. "I understand kid. I just got to ask you real quick, if you could please tell me what went on between you and the Gardensen kid. Waiter says he heard some kind of yelling going on…can you tell me what you two were talking about?"*Everybody has their goddamned price, Brian*…his words echoed in my head.

I leaned back against the bedpost and stared Officer Raymond straight in the eyes, keeping my voice as level as possible. I never once stuttered or looked away when the words left my mouth, the one lie I managed to tell convincingly over and over the next few months. "I don't remember what happened, Sir."

He stared at me, eyebrows raised.

I shook my head. "I don't remember anything at all."

*   *   *

A day later I was released from the hospital. The nurse and my mother walked us to a cab that had been called. A swarm of reporters were waiting for me at the door of the hospital. A security guard had to help clear the way for us to get through to the cab.

"Sir! Sir, is it true Charles Gardensen pulled a gun on you?!"

"Brian! What caused the fight between you and Mr. Gardensen?"

"Do you have any ideas of his whereabouts? He's been missing for two days now!"   "Have you had any contact with Charles Gardensen?"

"Is it true he attacked you? Do you plan on pressing charges?"

"Can you tell us anything? Please, sir, a minute of your time!"

My mother was flustered, "Brian, what is all of this?"

The cab driver stepped out and helped us both into the car. The security guard tried unsuccessfully to block reporters from banging on the windows and screaming questions at us. I watched the crowd of people become smaller and smaller as we drove away. "It's the beginning, mom. Try and get used to it."

*   *   *

I had the next month off from school, since it was the break between the first and second semester. That entire month was summed up in what felt like a thousand knocks on our ratty front door and a nonstop ringing phone. My mother sent them all away from me. "I don't remember," "I don't remember anything." I had said it so many times that after awhile it became true. I had gotten hit in the head pretty damn hard. It was completely plausible that I suffer some sort of memory loss. Why not?

I had trouble sleeping. I would often lay awake in bed at night, thinking of the times we had spent hanging out. How Charles opened my eyes to a life I had never known existed. I always wondered where he was, and was constantly watching the news for if they had found him yet. Something inside me believed the worst. That he had taken his own life, afraid to face the world after the truth about his family had surfaced. Part of me believed he was still out there, at some bar, in a ridiculous costume, hiding out, crashing parties, smoking cigars, drinking a crazily named drink with some beautiful girl on his arm. I watched the news every night for any updates on his disappearance, but an entire month went by without any word.

The day before I had to leave my mother's apartment and board a bus back to the University, we had a knock on the door. I was sitting on the couch, ignoring a bowl of cereal and my mother was brewing coffee.

"For God's sake, it's eight-thirty in the morning," my

mother muttered, pulling her robe tighter around her body. She walked over and peered through the hole. "Who is it?"

"I'm sorry to trouble you, Miss. I'm looking for Brian Walden."

She rolled her eyes before glancing over at me. I shook my head. She nodded. "I'm sorry; he's unavailable right now. If you have a message or a card or something, I'll be sure to pass it along." There was an unusual silence on the other side.

Then the man spoke again. "Okay, well, can you tell him Astin Gardensen had stopped by and wished to speak with him...and if he ever has a moment, to please give me a call on my direct cell?" She looked at me, eyes wide. I sat still on the couch, not believing my ears.

"I'll leave the number under your doormat." There was silence for a moment, and then I could hear slight movement on the other side of the door. Then footsteps. He was leaving. I turned off the television and walked quickly to the door. Gently moving my mother aside, I undid the three locks and quickly began walking down the hall. "Mr. Gardensen!" I called, adrenaline running through my body.

He heard me just as he got to the door, the sound of my voice stopping him in his tracks. He turned around and faced me. We stared at each other quietly for a moment, sizing each other up just as Charles and I had did when we first met. Here I was, a scraggly kid in a t-shirt and pajama pants. And here was Astin Gardensen.

He was not a large man, if I remember correctly. No, nowhere near as big and pompous as I expected the almighty Astin Gardensen to be. He was of medium height and medium build. But he carried an air of self-importance. His forehead was creased with lines, most likely caused from worry and stress over the years of his life. The edges of his short hair were slightly graying. He lips were formed in a tight line across his face. He seemed much older than his years. He was not a large man, but you could tell he was incredibly powerful, the way he took his time before speaking or doing anything. His silence was intimidating. He made me nervous.

"Mr. Gardensen," I spoke again, breaking the silence between us. "I'm Brian." When he didn't say anything, I put my hands in my pockets. "Would you like to come in?"

*   *   *

"Would you like a cup of coffee?" My mother asked, having changed out of her bathrobe and into one of her nice Sunday dresses in record time.

"No, thank you. I won't be staying too long." He informed us, sitting stiffly on the living room couch. He had a briefcase with him. I couldn't believe he was really sitting here in our living room. I stared at him, wanting to say so much and having no idea where to start either. He looked at me, as if experiencing the same feeling.

"I'm sorry for bursting in on you two at such an early hour in the morning, but I really didn't have any other time to do it." He spoke, leaning forward in his seat. "It's not a problem at all." I replied, softly.   He cleared his throat. "You'll have to forgive how uninformed I am about the situation between you and Charles. I understand you were friends?"

I nodded. "Yes. He was a good friend to me, Sir."
Astin nodded, his stony face not displaying any emotions. He was very businesslike, and very intimidating. Charles claimed he was very fatherly with Elijah, but it was hard for me to imagine the person in front of me as a jovial father. "I see. Well, to be honest, I can imagine a thousand reasons why a

fight would erupt between you and Charles. He certainly isn't the easiest person to get along with."

I remained silent, daring not to interrupt. "I was informed that you were injured and spent a few days in a hospital because of Charles. Is that true?"

I nodded.

"From what everyone tells me you claim to not remember a thing as to why Charles had assaulted you in the restaurant the night he disappeared?"

I hesitated, but it was only for a moment. "Yes sir, it's true. I don't remember why we fought. I...can't really remember anything from that night."

He stared at me for a few long hard seconds. I tried as hard as I could to keep my gaze steady, but he was far too strong for me. Within a few seconds, I broke away and began staring at the floor.

"I imagine you incurred quite a hospital bill, with the overnight stays and all."

I shrugged. "I honestly haven't given the hospital bill that much thought, Sir." I replied, rubbing the back of my neck. "To be honest, it's the last thing I'm worried about."

"Well, I would worry about it if I were you. I know you worked part-time at your school library and from what I know they don't have health insurance for part-timers. You spend an hour in the ER that's got to be at least three hundred dollars right there." He went on, ignoring me. He opened the briefcase and pulled out a checkbook. He was silent the entire time he wrote out the check. "How do you spell your last name, Brian?" He asked me, his pen poised carefully over the check.

"Walden, it's uh, W-A-L-D-E-N." I recited out carefully, as

Astin copied down the letters. "And this really isn't necessary, Sir. I promise. You don't have to-"

"Brian," he cut me off, and I could see where Charles learned that famous habit of his. "I apologize for whatever trouble Charles has caused you. I really do. I also really appreciate the fact that you've declined to press charges against him several times." He stood up and began walking towards our front door. I got up and followed him, realizing this was his way of letting me know he had to leave. "Most people would tell you you're crazy not to. But I truly appreciate it from the bottom of my heart. Our family has been through quite enough these past few years." He handed me the check. "I imagine Charles would attack his only friend and then flee from the scene would have to deal with some pretty serious issues from our family past. Issues we wouldn't want brought up again. So your memory loss, real or not, has been quite a blessing." He walked over to me and held out the check, face down. "You're a good kid. Take it easy, all right?" My hands remained at my sides. I didn't want to take his money.

"Take it," he said, his voice colored with the slightest hint of sternness. "It's the least I can do."

I took the check from his hands. He stared at the front door, when I realized he was waiting for me to let him out. I undid the locks and held the door open for him.

"Thank you for your time, Brian." He offered a brief smile. I nodded.

"Anytime, Sir."

"Do apologize to your mother for me, I haven't the time to say goodbye to her personally."

"Will do, Sir." He took a few steps before he stopped

and turned around. I was still standing at the door, watching him walk away, just like he knew I would be.

"You wouldn't happen to know where Charles is, would you?"

Ruefully, I shook my head.

He nodded. "Well, if you ever hear from him, or find out, please let us know. We just want him to come home. Okay? If you get a chance to speak with him at all, please tell him that."

I nodded. "I promise I will." He took one last look at me turned, walking out of our apartment building and out onto the street. He got inside a car, which was parked out front and waiting for him the entire time. The car peeled away and I never heard from or spoke to Astin Gardensen again.

My mother came out of her bedroom, her face fresh with makeup. "Is he gone?" she asked incredulously.

I nodded; feeling unexplainably exhausted all of a sudden. My mother noticed. "Are you okay, honey? You've gone all white."

I nodded. "I'm just really tired."

"You want to try and eat something?"

I shook my head. "I think I'm going to lie down."

She looked over my face, worriedly. "Okay..." she noticed the check, which was still in my hands, face down. "What's that?" I glanced down at it, forgetting it was in my hands. "It's a check he wrote me...he said it was for the hospital bills." I handed it to her and started walking towards my bedroom. She started screaming before I even got halfway there.

*   *   *

I went back to school the following semester and Charles was still a missing person. Another six months went by.

Nothing. My mother had used some of the money Astin had given us and moved out of our apartment on Stratton Street and into a bigger and much nicer apartment on the newly renovated side of town. Not Park Place, but definitely not Baltic Avenue anymore either.   I used some of the money Astin had given us and moved out of the University dorms into my own private studio apartment. No more roommates for me.

A few articles came out in the paper the following year. Some were on Charles Gardensen, and how the hunt for the son of the renowned tycoon was still going…some were on myself, the silent roommate who moved out into his own apartment to be left alone…many were on the divorce of Astin and Adele Gardensen. I can't say I was shocked. I wondered if Charles was still alive. I wondered if he was reading the papers and knew what had happened to his parents. To myself. I wondered how long it would take for him to realize he could come out of hiding, because I had kept his secrets to myself. There was no reason for him to really stay away, if he was still alive out there. No reason at all. But he didn't return. Years went by and nothing.

*   *   *

It's been twelve years since Charles and I met…yesterday I was awarded my PhD. My mother and Tara were at the ceremony. My mother cried. I was so relieved and exhausted and done with school, and Tara was thrilled. I had finally done it. I looked back on the years I had spent molding and shaping my life. They all led up to this moment. Dr. Walden. Dr. Brian Walden, M.D. I had made it. Even though we had already left Stratton Street and its rags behind, I was certain now that we'd never ever go back.

"I can officially say, I am married to a Doctor," Tara trilled, happily, on her fourth drink of the night. We were celebrating at the house. We had moved in with my mother a few years back, since she had the extra room and Tara was supporting both of us on her income as an Art teacher. As lame as it sounds, it made sense and my mother was only too thrilled to have us stay with her. She claimed to be too lonely in such a big house, and hinted that she'd love to have additions to the family. As soon as Tara got her Bachelor of Arts, we were married.

"It's a long way until Dr. Walden," I warned her, the night of our honeymoon. I ran my hands up and down her body, which had thickened up a little over the years, much to my liking. "Well, it just so happens I've got about four years I can spare," she giggled drunkenly, kissing my lips. "Actually, it's going to be about six or seven more years…"She laughed.

"Shut up, Brian. Just shut the fuck up." And that's exactly what I did for the next several hours. Tara had planned a surprise graduate party, inviting all my friends who were in the same medical program as I was. After a few drinks, we were all having a pretty good time. I stood against the backyard wall, smiling to myself. I was married to the only woman I had ever loved. I had just received the degree I had spent my life chasing after. Pretty soon Tara and I were going to move out into our own place, because well, as much as I love my mother, I was excited for us to have our privacy.

"Hey, anybody, hey, anybody want a Hairy Navel? Anybody?" my friend Gus started shouting out. His question was followed by a chorus of loud "YEAHS!"

"Good, good, great, 'cause I've got on right here." He said, lifting up the shirt of some guy standing next to him.

Loud laughter followed. The poor chubby unknown party-goer downed his beer quickly, pulling his shirt back down and looking embarrassed. I smiled to myself, the name of the drink triggering a memory of a night I had spent with Charles at some fancy club or other. The first time I had ever drank alcohol. *"I'll take a Hairy Navel," he said suavely to the waitress. "My friend here will have the Fuzzy Navel," he leaned closer towards her but made sure I could still hear him, "between you and me, he just isn't ready for that leap yet."*

"Baby, we're out of tequila!" Tara called the other side of the backyard. She was sitting with a bunch of her friends from the school she taught art at. She stood up but lost her balance and fell back into her seat, laughing.

"Are you sure you need any more, I think you've had quite enough," I teased, dropping a kiss on her head.

"No, it's not for me," she stared at me earnestly. "Not for me. For them." She pointed at her friends and then stared back at me, deadpan. They all began laughing.

"Right, right. Not for you, just for them. Okay then, I'll be right back," I said to them, winking at her. She winked back at me. God, I loved her. I strolled into the kitchen, humming to myself. I found a second bottle of tequila waiting on top of the kitchen counter, next to a newspaper. I couldn't help but take a look. It was a habit of mine; steadfastly born during the first days that Charles went missing. Throughout the first few months I had constantly been reading the papers or watching the news without any luck. Now I do both of those just because I'm so used to doing them both.

I quickly flipped through the first few pages and dropped it when nothing caught my attention. Under the newspaper was a letter from my Tara's parents. *"Congratulations, son!"*

it read. *"We knew you could do it. Don't forget the rest of the clan now, Dr. Walden."* I smiled. Her folks were just as wacky as she was. There was another letter underneath that one. I opened it. Another letter of congratulations from Tara's sister in Ohio. Another piece of mail underneath that. I opened it. Bill. I opened the next letter. Credit card offer. Cable bill. A memorandum from the school Tara taught at. I tossed it aside. Another piece of mail.

It was in a plain envelope, with no return address. I frowned, opening it. It was a small piece of paper, a bit faded. I recognized it in a second, my heart nearly stopping at the sight of it. It was a wrinkly little friendship coupon.

Good for One Random Visit!